D1565121

Signs and Wonders

Also by Roger Pinckney

Signs and Wonders

For Jeane with many thanks!

[signature]

ROGER PINCKNEY

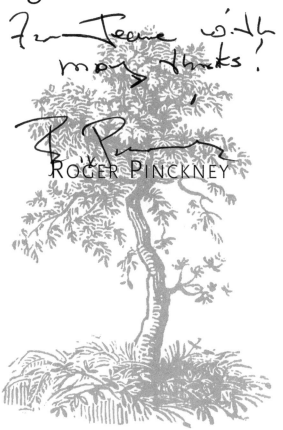

Wyrick & Company
Charleston

To Susan, my little blonde head,
my angel of shining light. Thanks again.

Published by Wyrick & Company
Post Office Box 89
Charleston, SC 29402

Designed by Sally Heineman

Printed in the United States of America

Library of Congress Cataloging-in-Publication Data

Contents

Preface

"A vain and adulterous generation seeketh after a sign," the Good Book says, "but unto them, no sign will be given." If I had time to look it up right now, I could tell you it's somewhere in Matthew, or maybe John. But wherever you might find it, it's as crushing a condemnation as you're likely to encounter in a book where there are more crushing condemnations than you can hardly stand.

But "Gawd use all-two he han'," a Gullah preacher told me one time. And I am here to testify the Lord is merciful above all things. In a lifetime of bumming from sunny ragged islands to the edge of the tundra, I have seen signs and wonders aplenty.

They have come to me in the greening bottomland timber and on the sunlight splintering on new snow. In the flare of a buck deer's nostrils, in the popping of barnacles, in the cries of wild geese, and in the scent of a woman in love. A thousand times ten thousand blessings, punctuated by gunfire and divorce and the occasional barroom brawl, blessings also, in strange and wonderful ways.

Down in the Bahamas there is a place called the Glass Window. It's where the island of Eleuthera, one hundred miles long and anywhere from ten miles to ten feet wide, narrows down to nothing and the surging North Atlantic rushes to meet the warm and fertile Caribbean. Wind and cliffs and booming surf, it is a place of astounding violence and beauty and it's easy to imagine the two oceans making whatever love they know how to make.

The Queen's Highway ran across a natural stone arch there in the old days. The ocean took that arch and a half-dozen bridges the Bahamians had erected over the years. The current bridge sits eleven feet out of kilter and the approaches are rutted and potholed and littered with boulders and no local will cross before checking for "rages"—freak waves sometimes one hundred feet high that loom up out of the sea, often without warning.

Way out to sea, you can sail right over a wave like that and never know it. It's just a bulge out on the deep blue and there isn't any trouble at all until something gets in the way. And that's the way this book started out, just a bulge, no trouble to nobody. And now you are squarely in the way.

If you don't like hunting and fishing, good food and good whiskey, sex and hoodoo, you probably won't like this book. If you don't love Jesus and beer joints where they sweep up the eyeballs at closing time, you probably won't like it either.

These are my stories, then. Some of them have been published in various magazines and you might recognize the ones which have not. They will take you, as they have taken me, from a boyhood bogging the salt creeks to a manhood on a hardscrabble northwoods farm, back again to the land that bore me, still lush and beautiful but fraught with politics, litigation and swindle as the last of the wild places go for second homes and golf courses and discount shopping malls.

They will take you north again after birds and big fish. And maybe they will teach you to find your own signs and wonders, however they may be given you.

The Moon in Three Phases

Driftwood Corey had a shack out where U.S. 21 crossed the Harbor River on the last leg of its transcontinental odyssey to the sea. There was a little island there, a quarter-acre remnant of an ancient beachline, with a few scrubby pines and one lonesome palmetto for shade. His front steps were a dozen yards from whizzing traffic and his back bedroom hung over the marsh on pilings.

He passed his days cruising the beach in an old military Dodge, an abused and rusted relic of our fathers' war, picking up whatever the wind had blown ashore. He varnished pallets and hatchcovers and sold them for coffee tables, took great chunks of driftwood, trimmed a branch here, rounded a knob there until they looked like women—naked mostly—then set them like bait along his porch railing. Tourists would slow and look. Once slowed, they stopped. Once stopped, they bought.

I met him midway through my tenth summer. I was bicycling home from the river, a stringer of fat and dull-eyed July mullet dangling from my handlebars. Seized with sudden thirst, I stopped at Koth's All Right Grocery for a Dixie Cola. Driftwood Corey was parked in the shade by the icehouse, peering under the hood of the Dodge, his bony hips and knobby elbows pointed skyward. He must have heard flapping fishtails as I wobbled by. He rose, turned and fixed me with blue-eyed radar.

"Hey, sonny," he yelled in an accent that I had never before heard, "come over and lend a man a hand."

I propped my bike against a tree, walked over and leaned across the loose and rusting fender. It sagged and buckled under my meager weight. Beyond was a steaming flathead engine, rumbling like a volcano about to blow.

A broken fanbelt lay where it had been slung, in a knot tightly wound around the brake cylinder. He was struggling with a new one, prying on the generator with a crowbar, vainly trying to secure it with a worn and splayed adjustable wrench. He bade me lean on the bar as he fought to turn a bolt, sweating, shaking, and uttering what I assumed to be curses—unintelligible words spit out like cockleburs. When we were finished, I asked, "Mister, where you from?"

He glanced at me briefly, those blue eyes vibrating. "From Ireland, sonny, where they're hanging men and women for the wearing o' the green."

"What's wrong with green?" I asked.

He looked at me with a mixture of disbelief and pity. "Its Eire, sonny, and Sinn Fein. The Brits have a price on me head. I zipped three of 'em in 1916."

That didn't make much sense, so I changed tack and asked a different question. "You work around here someplace?"

His face began to twitch and contort, his eyes rolled briefly back into his head. He went into a crouch, arms spread wide like a comic heavily burdened with a punchline. "Work? A man needs no work!" he shouted. "All a man needs is time to live!" He gave a mighty jump, his feet flying higher than the fender of his truck, threw out his hands, clicked his heels and shouted on the way down, "And a time to die!" He hit the ground on the tips of his toes, spun around once and threw himself onto his back like he had been struck down by lightning. He lay there for an instant, his eyes closed and the thinnest of smiles playing across his lips, then winked at me and leapt to his feet again. "Aye, it was a rough time, sonny," he said as if the conversation had not been interrupted by his spasmodic acrobatics, "the women a-cryin' for the boys who died with Parnell. And me in a pile of bricks with that long-barrelled Luger. I made it plenty hot for them."

He might as well have been speaking Greek. But I remembered "Sinn Fein," and that night looked it up in the encyclopedia. It was one of those words that wasn't spelled like it sounded, but I finally found it after twenty minutes of flipping pages. It said "we, ourselves" and told of the Irish and their six-hundred-year struggle for freedom. And so I counted myself proud. I knew a genuine Irish revolutionary, vintage 1916; maybe even a hero.

But I soon learned he had told Tommy he was a graduate of Harvard School of Law and, later in the same one-sided conversation, that he had recently retired from the Mayo Clinic. I tried hard to incorporate all three stories into a single biography, struggling with it for months.

That all came later. Right then, I was still on my bike in the parking lot of the All Right Grocery. Joe Smalls and Meatball Jenkins had few doubts about Driftwood Corey—they knew he could throw the root and cast the evil eye. Meatball, the three-hundred-pound gas, ice, and carry-out man, had his face to the grocery store glass, watching the goings-on. Out on the Bay Street curb, Joe waited behind the wheel of the Broad

River Seafood truck, refusing to come any closer. Only when the old man had dropped the hood, mounted a seat leaking springs and stuffing, and disappeared in a cloud of smoke and gear clash, would either of them make a move.

Meatball came outside, an icepick in one hand, shaking the other like he was trying to sling water off it. "Ooh, that man—that man he hex you—praise Jesus. Ooh Sweet Jesus, keep that root away from me."

It wasn't often a Negro would talk about the root. Some didn't believe and were afraid you'd remember their parents did. Some did believe and were just afraid.

I cut a sharp circle with the bike and tossed a question at Meatball as he headed for the icehouse. "What you mean, Meatball? Root ain't going to hurt you."

Meatball stopped in midstride, considered briefly what I had said. "That may be right, boy. But root is like ghost. Ghost ain't goin' hurt you neither. You is goin' to hurt yoself gettin' out the way."

I fell in behind, dogging his tracks on the bike, trying to get him to tell me more about island voodoo. But he had said nearly everything he would, and temporarily ended the conversation with a warning. "You stay clear of that man! You ever see a man jump and carry on like that? Oh, Sweet Jesus, keep that root away from me!"

I knew about the root——those secret ingredients sewed up in a little burlap wad. There were white roots like the Money Root and the Follow Me Boy Love Charm that were big hits on Saturday nights. And then there were blue roots that would cause cows to get sick, chickens to stop laying, wells to throw sand.

The evil eye was worse yet. While a blue root might make a man wish he were dead, the evil eye could put him in his grave. First off, his throat would swell till he couldn't eat or drink. Then he'd take to his bed and the hags would roost on his bedposts and take turns riding him to death. Captain Jack Chaplin died like that, sweating and bucking, they said, like there was a woman on top of him.

The root and the evil eye were the domain of the root doctor, a practitioner whose badges of office included blue sunglasses and a black Lincoln car. A blue root might be buried on the victim's land—beneath the steps worked best—so the unfortunate would pass over it many times a day. As an alternative, the root doctor could chew a root, circumnavigating his prey seven times, staring, working his mouth, and mumbling unknown tongues, the root juice running down his chin.

A white man cut a wide circle around a root doctor. A black man crossed over to the other side of the street when he saw one coming.

Joe ground the truck into reverse. Meatball met him at the icehouse door, still slinging his hand, cussing and praying in spurts. "Ooh, that man," he said again.

Joe swung down from the cab, caught the last of Meatball's utterances. "Ain't no man," he said with the utmost certainty. "He the plateye."

The plateye was the most dreaded of the spirits that flitted around the edges of island reality, the mere mention of which was too much for Meatball. He could do no more than work his lips and swallow.

I took momentary advantage of Meatball's loss of words. "Ain't no plateye," I said. "He said he's from Eire or someplace."

Joe briefly tolerated my ignorance. "Shit," he said. "What you know 'bout the plateye?"

Meatball went to work with the pick, whittling huge blocks of ice into manageable pieces, which Joe wrestled into the dark of the stinking truck.

"That's right," he said, finally. "Ain't nobody know the plateye. He come clean through tin roof. Git you no matter what."

"Plateye don't drive no truck," I said.

Joe snorted. "Boy, you is downright dumb," he said. "Plateye do anything he want."

I tried to say something else, but Meatball cut me off. "You shut up, boy, or he'll git you, for sho'."

And so I left them there, laboring over the ice, shaking their heads and mumbling. I pedalled homeward, fish tails and fins keeping rhythm on bicycle spokes, little drops of fish slime and sea water marking my passing in the Carolina dust.

Then, in my sixteenth spring, there came one of those miserable Saturdays in early March, a Saturday when a buzzard could die of boredom. A mean northeaster had been blowing for a week, keeping us indoors and all but the most desperately mortgaged fishermen off the river. A late morning break in the weather found me heading for the beach to see what the storm had driven ashore.

Tommy drove his Jeep. Like Driftwood Corey's Dodge, it was a leftover from the war, patched, puttied and painted Rustoleum red. There was no cab, no windshield, no muffler, and we checked the gas by dipping a stick down the filler spout.

Those eighteen miles seemed to take forever. We labored up the bridge across the first big river, rattled and whined down the pocked and wrinkled blacktop, by sandy field and pungent marsh, beneath spreading and brooding oaks, their branches all dripping with mournful Spanish moss, then over the last long causeway as the highway kept its rendezvous with the sea. Finally, there was the old abandoned lighthouse above the distant piney treeline, and the smell of the salt sea on the roadwind.

Driftwood's Dodge was backed to his porch, loaded with a great pile of gnarled and twisted trunks, stumps, and branches. We didn't see him, but we hooted, hollered and revved the engine as we passed.

We broke out of the woods onto the beach and, as we expected, found the tracks of his old Dodge upon the sand. We parked just above the high tide mark, began walking, looking for things he had missed.

The tide was way down, dead low, just hovering and fluttering on the edge of flood. Tommy walked the edge of the water while I patrolled where hightide surf had rolled into the oak and palmetto thickets.

The picking was good. Right away I found a bunch of glass floats, the kind Japanese net fishermen use. They were blue from incessant sunlight, big as grapefruit, strung together on a long piece of manila line, in those days worth an easy ten-spot in the Savannah antique stores. Then, I found an almost new beer cooler, minus the top. I soon tired of dragging my treasures, so I set the cooler in the sand and tied the floats to a careening branch, lest I forget them on my way back to the Jeep. As it happened, I would never see them again.

I was just putting the final twist in the rope when I saw an odd shape poking from the iridescent green of springtime cassena. I wrestled loose a wooden crutch.

It was handmade of sapling willow, carefully split, bent and fastened with brass screws. The arm pad and grip were covered with ship's canvas lashed down with fine wire, palm-polished but just starting to show rust. I didn't know what to make of it.

There was a whistle from down by the water. I wore glasses, which nearly always bore a patina of dust, dried sweat, and salt spray. I blinked and squinted across the sand. Tommy was carrying a square green bottle, the kind good scotch comes in.

"Got a knife?" he yelled.

I worked it from my pocket. "What the hell you got?"

"It's a note," he said. "A message in a bottle!" With trembling hands he cut through tape, levered out a cork sealed with red candle wax. He shook a rolled up note out onto the sand. "Where the hell did you get that crutch?"

"Snaked it out of the brush. What's that note say?"

Tommy unrolled it carefully. The paper was wet but it had been written in pencil, so it was still legible. I looked over his shoulder as he read. "Ship *India Star*. Fourteen days out of Liverpool. Poor Stumpy lost overboard. God rest his soul."

Shivers worked on me like cold drizzling rain. "It's Stumpy's crutch. Poor bastard's fallen overboard and drowned."

Tommy whistled. "I'll bet he's up the beach somewhere."

I looked north and south. I could see a half-mile in either direction before the sea spray closed in and made everything smoky and gray. I said, "Maybe the sharks ate him."

The drizzling shivers went to work on Tommy, too. He said, "This business gives me the willies. Let's get the hell out of here." But then he looked out to where the surf was curling and lapping onto the sand and after a minute said, "Tide's changed. Let's stick the note back in the bottle, write one of our own about finding Stumpy's crutch and throw it back."

"That'll never work," I said. "Remember the time we dropped all those bottles off the bridge? We put our addresses in 'em and promised to send a dollar to anybody who wrote. They didn't get ten miles. We still owe Julian Caldwell twelve bucks."

He thought about that for a few seconds, then licked his finger and held it above his head. "The wind's switched. Let's go back to the store, buy one of them kites they sell to the Yankee kids. We'll lash the bottle to Stumpy's crutch, hook it up with a piece of fishing line, let the kite tow it. It'll go a hundred miles."

It seemed the thing to do, something ceremonial and ridiculous, something maudlin and predictably sixteen. And so we decided to nobly spread the news of poor Stumpy's death to an indifferent world. We emptied our pockets and found we had nearly five dollars between us, quite a bit in those days— enough for kite and string, with something left over for sweet rolls and Dixie Colas.

Driftwood Corey had been busy while we were on the beach, having gathered bleached stumps and trunks, wave-blasted hatch covers, pallets and timbers, and made great piles at the corners of his porch. He was trudging across the yard, lugging a creation resembling a seven-foot ballerina with one huge onion of a breast, as we whined and jostled by in the Jeep. We waved and whistled, but he kept to his work, never looking in our direction.

The store was on the first piece of high ground west of the river, a tin-roofed, two-story building with the store on the ground floor and the house upstairs, vending whatever a person needed to survive on the islands—bait and tackle, day-old bread, canned vegetables, frozen steaks, chops and stew meat, rotten chicken necks for crabbing, mosquito spray, sunburn cream, snakebite kits, cold beer, and soda. There were gas pumps in front and stinking gator pens out back where Yankees could peer for a dollar a head.

The kites were put away until summer, but we found them and pulled out a flag-colored model bearing a dusty picture of the Masked Marvel. I grabbed a spool of fishing line, a box of chocolate Moon Pies and two Dixie Colas. We had thirty-seven cents left—just enough for the quart of oil the Jeep would likely consume on the way home.

We drove upwind of the gator pens, ate the Moon Pies and drank the colas. I had a steady hand, so I worded the note, keeping it simple: "Found this note in this bottle and Stumpy's crutch. March 1962, Hunting Island, S.C." Then we signed our names. Tommy rolled it up and carefully pushed it into the bottle from the *India Star* and we turned again seaward.

A great smoky pillar was rising to meet us. It rolled and billowed above the marsh, sliding east on the wind. There were three fires in Driftwood Corey's yard. We slowed to a crawl, looked long and hard at the flames. One had burned to a pile of ashes that flickered blue and green tongues from sea mineral, the others blazed yellow and hot.

"What the hell's he up to?" I asked.

Tommy shrugged, slid the Jeep back into gear. "Cleaning up, I reckon."

On the beach again, I lashed the bottle to the crutch while Tommy unrolled the kite, put the cross sticks together, and stretched the paper over the little slots at the corners. The wind had stiffened since the tide change. In less than a minute, the kite was a hundred feet overhead, whipping and tugging in the gusts. I let out the rest of the line, walked down to the edge of the surging sea, stopping just before the water came to the tops of my shoes. I laid the crutch in the wave wash, knowing the next breaker would float it free.

We stood on the beach and watched as our little vessel cleared the foaming backwash, as it staggered across the first curling breaker, as it cleared the swells a hundred yards off the beach. We watched until we could no longer see the crutch, only the Masked Marvel tugging at the long length of line. In time, everything was lost in the gray mist from the wrinkling ocean.

And we stood there a minute longer. "So long, Stumpy," Tommy said.

The smoke rolling up from Driftwood Corey's had changed color. It hung in long black greasy strands in the tops of the pines in the island backwoods. Every so often we'd catch a whiff of it in the roadwind. It smelled of sulfur and pitch, of burning rags.

About the third time we winded it, Tommy pushed the gas to the floor. The engine hesitated, stumbled, then slowly began to pick up speed. He yelled, the wind pulling the words from his mouth, "His house is on fire!"

The speedometer had never worked, so I cannot tell you how fast we got that Jeep rolling, but I know it was way faster than it was ever intended to go. The exhaust was roaring, the steering wheel hammering in Tommy's hands, tires and gears whining in hellish harmony, the devil wind snatching at jackets and hats.

Tommy was right. Flames had eaten off half the porch, were gnawing up the north wall, working toward the tarpaper roof. Thick white smoke was rolling from the windows.

We slid to a stop, and hit the ground running.

Smoke hung in a thick layer just below the ceiling. It cut at the back of my throat, made my eyes water till I could barely see. I heard Tommy in front of me, "Get on your knees! Get below the smoke!" I fought for breath, and bellowed for Driftwood.

Tommy found him in a rocking chair in the middle of his living room, sitting with eyes closed, slowly rocking as his house burned. He had a leg lock on a bottle of Old Setter.

I crawled up to him, grabbed a knee. His pale blue eyes snapped open and he looked at me without seeing.

Tommy rose to a crouch, grabbed him and shook him hard. "Come on, Driftwood, you've got to get out of here!"

But Driftwood kept his eyes shut. His head wobbled like one of those fuzzy little dogs in the back window of a Mexican's car.

Tommy was a good man in a tight spot. He said, "Grab one side of the rocker and we'll drag this crazy bastard outside."

The rocker bottoms slid easily across the footworn floor, but the armrests would not clear the door. We fought it for a moment, on our knees on the porch, the fire fairly licking at our elbows. Our bumping, scraping, and swearing roused Driftwood Corey. He took the bottle from between his knees, and took one long, last hard pull from it, the pull he was probably saving for the end. Then Tommy shoved him back into the smoke, crawled around behind him and tipped the chair forward in the doorway.

The old man hit the porch, rag-doll limp, and rolled down the steps out into the yard. But he came up fighting like a neckbroke cat, trying to get back into the house. Tommy tackled him. I grabbed a leg and hung on. When he realized he couldn't slip loose, he began hollering. "My mattress! My mattress! I gotta go get my mattress!"

We let him go and he led us around back, out to where the shack hung over the marsh. He pointed to a window. It was a ways from the flames, so Tommy and I slithered in.

We found the mattress. There was a woman on it. With covers up to her chin and eyes wide open, she stared up at the tendrils of smoke that were just beginning to curl overhead. We figured we'd have another wrestling match, but she got right out of bed when she heard Driftwood out in the marsh.

She was maybe sixty, dressed in jeans and a flannel shirt, and was as weathered, lined and gray as any of those creations just sent up in smoke. Tommy grabbed her by the elbows and funneled her through the window, and Driftwood eased her to the ground. I could smell piss and stale whiskey, even through the smoke and smothering air.

She and Driftwood cried and slobbered over each other. He put his arms around her, petted her, called her Baby. She put her face in the hollow of his neck and blubbered.

In fifteen short minutes, there was nothing left of the shack but a knee-high pile of white-hot ashes. And there was nothing for us to do but give them a ride back to town.

We dropped them off on the west end of Bay Street bridge,

drunk, dirty, and as far as I know, flat broke. There was a narrow alleyway there, running past the old cotton ginnery down to the shrimp docks. The town's only pay telephone was there, too, along with a couple of Coca-Cola machines. The island Negroes hung around there on Saturday afternoons, killing time, socializing, some nipping the moonshine they bought behind the cab stand, waiting for rides that would take them across the bridge and home, or the other way to the Savannah juke joints.

Somebody gave a whoop, then the crowd seemed to congeal into little knots, speculating, no doubt, about those fool white people in that beat-up Jeep. When they recognized Driftwood Corey and when they saw Tommy signal a turn, they cleared a broad path before us, parting like the waters before Moses.

When we drove away there were just three people there— Driftwood Corey, Miss Baby, and a man talking on the pay phone. He was light-skinned, probably from up north somewhere, and maybe didn't know about the root and the evil eye.

I thought about that Saturday for months, pondering as when I had tried to accommodate all those divergent biographies years before. Some things, though, seemed certain. Driftwood Corey became to me no more than a common drunkard, a liar, and quite possibly a lunatic, as well. I no longer believed he was an Irish revolutionary still hiding from the British. I no longer had any time for stories about him once being a doctor or a lawyer. I laughed when I heard the Negroes whisper when he walked by.

I was not to see him again for ten full years. I graduated from high school, got married, won a scholarship to a major university, moved away further than I had ever been or even dreamed of going. Things went well for a while, then my marriage began to unravel and along with it, my brain.

I violated a trust I had attested was sacred. I met her in a bar where the art students hung out. She had been to Swiss boarding schools and had spent summers following her father around archaeological digs in the Middle East. I loved her because she wore a gold ring with an image of the mother goddess and told me stories about the ruins of Troy. I amused her because I was born on an island and spoke with an accent she had heard only in the movies. She summoned me whenever desire overcame her and she would ride me down until the bed broke beneath us.

Nobody knew but us.

But it was way, way too much. Mauled by lust and guilt, I fled south one Christmas vacation. I hung my clothes in my in-laws' back bedroom and tried to learn, once again, how to sleep with my wife.

Two days later, I ran into Tommy in one of those dark and windowless bars where it always seemed midnight. We lined bottles on the table while I, hanging on words, vainly groped at the ghosts of lost years. Our rambling conversation finally struck upon Driftwood Corey.

Tommy's face lit up. "Oh yes," he said. "He's still around, living in that shack on the old fuel dock."

"Look here, Tommy," I said, "It's most Christmas. Let's find that old bastard. Let's take him a jug."

Boat traffic on the Intracoastal Waterway stopped at the fuel dock before they built the new marina further downriver. There was a shack out on the end, unused for decades, that formerly kept the dockmaster out of the weather while he wrote up invoices for gas, diesel, and before that, cordwood for river steamers. We saw a haggard face at the back window, heard a scraping chair, the chair falling over, and then Driftwood Corey stepped out to meet us.

His face had weathered like wave-beaten pine, but his eyes still shone with that old blue fire and he still walked like there were springs coiled beneath his feet. If he remembered us as the ones who had foiled his suicide that stormy Saturday so long ago, he gave no indication of it, fixing his attention instead upon the bottle of Old Setter beneath my arm.

"Evening, Driftwood," I said. "Merry Christmas."

"And a merry, merry Christmas to you, sonny," he said in that cocklebur brogue. He eyed the bottle, and once he had it in his hands, stroked it like it had fur or feathers. He grinned with gratitude and lunacy, his eyes vibrating like that first time we met.

And like that first morning, I was at a loss for conversation. "Making enough to get by?" I inquired.

It was the wrong question to ask. I saw something indescribable flash across his face, and his mouth began to twitch and quiver. Tommy saw it coming, too, and braced himself.

"All a man needs," Driftwood Corey hollered, "is time to live!" Then he added a new twist. He hooked a thumb into the rope that held up his britches and gave them a mighty shake. They rolled and flapped around his skinny hips and legs. "A man can only wear one pair of pants at a time!" And then he shook a bony finger in my face and to my utmost amazement shouted, "And a man can only love one woman at a time!"

Before I could react to the lightning he sent through me,

he leapt into the air, in a jump worthy of a basketball player. He tried to click his heels but since he was barefoot, they made only a swishing sound as callous met callous. On his way down he bellowed, "And a man needs a place to die!" He hit the hard deck with the point of his left hip, and rolled like he had training in judo. He flipped onto his back, stretched out, closed his eyes, and, clutching the bottle to his chest, grew a smile that looked like it had been massaged there by an undertaker.

I bent over him, looking down in a mixture of wonderment and confusion, when he opened one pale blue eye and winked.

River Song

Lee Webb was waxing philosophical over his after-work whiskey. Beek, Eddie, Jim and I were hustling around the house, digging out bedding, lanterns, and fishing rods for another expedition to Capers Island.

"My buddy so-and-so," Lee was saying, "told me his boy was going Up North to college. But he wasn't worried. He says everybody comes back to Beaufort."

Lee was Beek's daddy, an honorary uncle to the rest of us. His easy manner and succinct articulation compelled attention when we wouldn't listen to our own kin. We ceased preparations to catch a bit of that Friday evening wisdom.

"I told him his boy won't come back to Beaufort." Lee paused for a sip, then motioned toward the slice of wrinkling blue water just outside his living room window. "But he'll come back to that river."

Even at sixteen, we understood.

I got my first boat on my twelfth birthday, a battered cypress bateau. I scraped, caulked, and painted, soon mastered its oars, and learned subtle eccentricities of wind and tide on my weekly trips to Goat Island, a whole two miles across the Beaufort River. Just two years later, Jim, Eddie, Beek and I were spending nearly every weekend twenty miles downriver on Capers Island—a tenuous stretch of windblown dunes and brushy hummocks under continuous assault from the thundering surf.

There was a camp on the back side of Capers, cobbled of pallets, washed-up timber, and purloined plywood. For two years we fished spottail bass along the front beach, bogged for oysters, shot marsh hens in the tall cordgrass while we longed for mallards. Those were magic times, the wind rattling in the palmettoes, fish frying on the Dixie No Smoke, Beek plucking away at his banjo, the river forever singing its sad background harmony.

Jim's daddy owned Capers, having inherited it from his father before him. Grandpa had bought it—the story went—for nineteen dollars in tax arrearage back when Teddy Roosevelt was president. But when ocean-front lots on Hilton Head hit a quarter-million dollars each, the temptation to sell became overpowering. We found ourselves dispossessed.

The Old Glory Hole lay just across the frothy inlet from Capers, a ramshackle collection of sagging tin roofs in a tangle of salt scrub on the south end of Pritchard's Island. But it was heaven. There were ducks, deer and wild hogs to hunt, a generator, a well, even a shower, and the best fishing any of us had ever seen. Buddy Lubkin and Zoo Von Harten were High Priests, inveterate river rats who had spent decades upon that Holy Ground. They knew all the intimacies of time and river, and shared them graciously, if impatiently. But they worked us unmercifully, relentlessly, inquiring, "Boy, is your leg broke?" whenever our chores did not meet their expectations of timeliness. Sixteen and chafing, we were soon searching for more congenial environment.

We found it on August 15, 1963—an obscure and brushy

hummock on a tortuous creek behind Bay Point Island, just inside the wild and plunging Gale Break surf. Jim was first ashore, striding up the bank like some ancient explorer about to claim new ground for his king. Eddie, Beek and I followed. The surf was mumbling off in the distance, cicadas singing their late summer song, heatwaves rippling, wrinkling the air. The low-tide gnats set upon us in a frenzy. We swatted and scratched, delivered a unanimous opinion. "It would take damn fools to build here."

A week later, we were back with our first load of two-by-fours. Upon whose land did we build? We knew not. A trip to the courthouse indicated that slight rise in the windswept marsh had apparently been overlooked by surveyors. Perhaps it could be deemed attached to the nearest high ground—Bay Point Island. Perhaps it was technically marsh, and thus public property. We sought to take advantage of ambiguity, fantasizing we might someday own it by simple possession.

In time, the Gale Break Camp boasted all the river camp amenities—a shaky dock over the shoe-sucking mud, electricity when the generator worked, heat when it wasn't too cold, running water whenever it rained. The log tells all. October 30, 1964: "Came down in Beek's boat, went striking and killed 2 bass. Went deer hunting, got a shot but missed." November 13, 1964: "Roger holed his boat in Port Royal Sound—almost lost it. Had crab for supper. Generator quit at ten. Went to bed early. Shrimp for breakfast." December 18, 1964: "Eddie used the log pencil for a plug in his shotgun magazine, so this is written three weeks late...."

In the early spring of 1965, I was pulled aside by my high school principal. What were my plans for college? Local, of course. He demanded an explanation. "I want to stick around a while," I stammered, "I got this camp at Gale Break..." Having never laid eyes on Gale Break, he thought it a terrible waste.

The last entry, the final page of a stained and dog-eared notebook, is dated August 29, 1966. The generator had run amok, fried the lights. But the full moon, it noted, was beautiful. "Look for the new edition coming soon" was written inside the back cover.

But alas, there was never a new edition. Beek was in the Coast Guard, Eddie in the Navy ROTC at Ole Miss, Jim at Georgia Tech. And Bay Point Island had a new owner, a prosperous local truck farmer who offered a lease for a dollar a year. We were three years short of the magic seven that may have given us claim by common law. We argued, equivocated, and did not sign.

I had run out of courses at the local college, and was off in Columbia, pecking away at a degree in English, making it home most weekends. While I labored toward graduation, a Saudi nobleman, seeking safe anchorage for his sea-going yacht, was casting lustful eyes upon Bay Point. His Royal Highness, being not universally esteemed, required a wide security zone around his royal personage. The inconvenience of our little camp was quickly remedied with a gallon of gas and a single kitchen match.

I made a final trip to Bay Point one rainy day in February 1970, bushed by signs warning against trespass, and stood weeping in the ashes of my boyhood.

In time I found other water, ten thousand cool jewel lakes in the Minnesota woods, the ice-rimmed, wind-torn shore of

Lake Superior, rivers that flowed north to the great Arctic Sea. There is magic there, too, booming ice at freeze up, deer and bear creeping to drink at water's edge, loons crying in the night as the aurora flashes and rolls overhead like silent tongues of Pentecostal fire.

The moon moves wolves in the piney timber and great skeins of Canada geese across the midnight sky. But the lakes lie impassive, oblivious to its pull. I lie awake some nights, feel it moving my salty blood, that old river song still reeling in the back of my brain.

Lee Webb was right. I watch another moonrise in wonder.

Mono and Me

It was a little after lunch and the pike were way down deep. We blubbered above them, bucking the wind in a fourteen-foot Alumacraft with a vintage six-horse OMC. Lots of line out, split shot like beads on the leaders, fighting to hold the spinners down where the fish were. The swivels were not working like they did in the store. Sixteen-pound mono wrapped until it looked like a long and skinny blue licorice twist.

This was way up in Minnesota, too far from salt, where the rivers run north like rivers are not supposed to do. Where I got stranded when my truck broke down on my way to Alaska. Where I wintered over and fixed the truck and by spring was too broke to leave.

The first fish hit as we rounded a long and rocky point all studded with tamarack and red cedar. I idled down, let the wind stop the boat. The fish ran up on the line like pike sometimes do. He saw me about the time I saw him.

He was as long as my arm and as big as my leg and the drag never had a chance to work at all. The mono, maxed from twisting, lasted about fifteen seconds. I wrung the throttle, cut out into deeper water, tied up another spinner, made another pass, got another strike, lost another fish.

Five pike were wearing my spinners like punk-rock jewelry before the first was flopping in the bottom of the skiff.

The joys of mono!

I was born in Beaufort County, South Carolina, and came of age with Daddy's Penn 209. Daddy liked his trout and puppy drum and spottails as well as anybody, but after twenty-odd years building docks and bridges and seawalls, you couldn't get him into a fishing boat for a salary. I was down with some childhood ailment—mumps or measles or chicken pox—when he walked into my bedroom and laid that Penn on the covers.

It wasn't much to look at, the plastic dull and weather-checked and the brass starting to grow green hair. But it was a genuine Penn, and I liked to cried. I lay there in bed and got after the corrosion with a patch of Momma's Brillo, doped the bearings with her Singer sewing machine oil. Up and around a few days later, I went down to Coastal Carolina Hardware, spooled up with 24-pound Dacron and pawed through the rods until I found one I could afford. It wasn't much to look at either, solid fiberglass the color of a Coke bottle, six feet, heavy as hell, about as responsive as a fence post.

And then I broke out the oars and hit the river. First in a twelve-foot skiff—a bateau, we say down here—and later in a sixteen-foot Yellow Jacket molded plywood runabout with a Johnson eighteen, in a twelve-year campaign from St. Helena Sound to Hilton Head. I swam with gators and sharks. I got struck by lightning. I fell overboard. I was swamped and marooned and cast ashore, a thousand times scared-to-Jesus-death, shot at, but never hit. Along the way, I caught redfish, bluefish and blackfish. I caught sheepshead and spadefish and stingrays as big as your kitchen table. I caught lots of fish, I caught a few fish, and sometimes I caught no fish at all. But I never lost a single fish from a broken line.

Never.

I wore that Penn slap out. The bearings got gravely. The levelwind keeled over and died. Finally, out on Port Royal Sound, I smoked the drag on a big bottom-hugging drum.

I was sporting the girls by then and laying back dimes and dollars for burgers and Pabst Blue Ribbon and Dixie Deluxe condoms, three for a quarter in packets bearing a Confederate flag and the hopeful words, "The South Shall Rise Again." I had this lively filly down in Savannah for the evening, heading for River Street where they'd draw you a brew if you were tall enough to slide your money over the bar. But on the way, I just had to breeze through Cranman's, in those days the biggest sporting goods store in east Georgia.

The girl pouted while I prowled the aisles and came across this slick little Garcia 302. It was a left-handed model, just like me, before some Einstein finally figured a reel could be ambidextrous if you could just swap the crank around to the other side. A hapless clerk thought he ordered a dozen J-6 Champions and a single left-handed Garcia. It turned out to be the opposite.

This was 1964, and no self-respecting salt water fisherman would come near an open-faced spinning reel. So Cranman's hooked them to generic fiberglass rods, and took a beating at twenty bucks each. I bought the Garcia for me and a Cherry Coke for the girl.

And then I dropped her on her front steps.

It was, I believe, the first spinning rig in Beaufort County. None of this Abu business, but a fine French Garcia, belying the notion that France is only capable of producing exquisite wine, automobiles prone to malfunction, and nuclear fallout in Polynesia. It was a beauty, too, with another spool pre-wound with the company's own choice of instant aggravation in a cute little waterproof can with the Garcia logo.

All of a sudden, I was a sportsman! I fished fish, not water. I could cast a three-quarter-ounce yellow bucktail thirty yards with a flick of the wrist. *Ploop* right in front of a snooping snook, a darting sea trout, an otherwise unflappable flounder.

But I soon found that monofilament had its eccentricities. It backlashed with artistic integrity. It got brittle from sunlight. You couldn't tell it was bad till it broke. And worst of all, its memory exceeded a quail hunter's nostalgia. If it was straight, nothing would make it happy until it was straight again. If it was coiled, it would not rest until it coiled back up. If it was tied....

Jack Bollack, friend and riverman, tried to weave a cast net of the stuff. Sleep overcame him 1,500 knots into the project. He left the net on the kitchen table, planning to take it up again after breakfast. Jack slept, but the mono did not. Daylight brought a snarl of monstrous proportions, a great torrent of profanity, and a quick trip to the backyard trashcan.

I read all the magazines. You know, the "Tips from Sportsmen" slot where you'd get a subscription and twenty-five bucks for figuring out how to tie mono so it wouldn't work loose. There was a new knot just about every month. So I tied my own—clusters of clove hitches that worked no better than anybody else's.

One blustery day found mono and me way out of our league—up to my waist in the plunging Pritchard's Island surf. My buddies and I had crawled up in a fishcamp on the south end named The Old Glory Hole. Our host and mentor, Old Man Buddy Lubkin—garrulous, barrel-bellied connoisseur of Black Label beer—was twenty feet away when I tied into a big spottail. Fond of his three-ought Senator, his 36-pound Dacron, and his flagpole rod, he was eyeing my puny efforts. When the fish found strength in the backwash and I slacked off on the drag, the old man's skepticism turned to profane disbelief. "What the hell you doin'?" he asked. I replied with the obvious: "I'm playing the fish."

"Play with him when you get him on the bank, son," he said. "Reel his ass in!"

I grew up and older and wound up in the Land of Ten Thousand Lakes, the Land of Ten Million Broken Lines. Misery loves company, in salt water or fresh water. With the Garcia and a boatload of fellow sufferers, I set out after largemouth late one sunny August Sunday. It was supposed to work like this: big bass would slip into the warm shallows to feed at sunset. We would be ready with frogs. Hook 'em through the pelvis, tether 'em to a thirty-inch leader. A slip sinker kept froggy bobbing in one spot until a bass picked him up.

August bass are a bit more circumspect than May's plug-sucking tail-walkers. They would lip a frog leg, consider it, mouth it, savor it, swim off aways, and get comfortable before dining. Watch the jibbling rod tip, slip the bail, watch coils upon coils of that damn mono slip into the dark water. Count to ten, to twenty, to eternity. Flip the bail, rear back on the rod and you got five pounds of bass with a hook in his lip and ten pounds of weeds on his snout.

Snap!

Monday morning, I walked into the local sports shop with

my Garcia and sad stories. The shopkeeper—like his cohorts everywhere—was an expert on everything with fins, fur, or feathers. He closed one eye, squinted like a pawnbroker through the other. "How old's this line?"

I had to admit I had no idea.

He laughed, stripped the reel and reloaded it with the same stuff that wrapped up and cost me all those pike. And when I was back with another sad tale, he looked at the rod tip, pronounced it worn, and reached for his sidecutters.

"Wait," I said. "Don't cut that rod!"

"Why not?"

And I thought to tell him about that pouting beauty there in Cranman's so long ago, a girl, surely a mother now and maybe even a grandmother, about Old Man Buddy Lubkin, gone but not ever forgotten, about the greasy heaving sea, the ragged surf on the outer bars, the hog reds running in the backwash, the copper sky when the sun slips down the west. I wanted to tell him all of this, but I knew he would not understand.

So I just looked at him, and he looked at me and said, "Wait a minute, Pinckney, I got just the thing for you." He disappeared into the back of the store. There was a shuffling of cardboard and a clatter of bait buckets and he came back with a long whippy piece of graphite and a Penn 209. "Some fool ordered this," he said, blowing the dust off the spool, "and never picked it up."

"Load her up with two hundred yards of 24-pound braided," I said.

"Two hundred yards? What kind of fishing are you gonna do?"

I just grinned and caressed the Penn while the past rolled over me like Pritchard's Island surf. Daddy smiled and Buddy Lubkin smiled and I knew right then, I was going home.

Highway 61, Revisited

South of Hastings, the trees play out; burr oaks and cotton-woods and willows, clustered now on hilltops and in bottoms, seem islands in an ocean of grass. Whitewashed barns ride the distance like ships on the high-heaving green. US 61 runs south and sometimes east and always downhill, to the river and to the sea.

We seek the sea, this road, this river and I. I am leaving Minnesota, going back to the sunny islands of my birth.

Bob Dylan, no stranger to this blacktop, wrote a song about it. "Lord, where you want this killin' done? Lord says out on Highway 61."

Highway 61 did not kill me, but it brought me here and Minnesota made a man out of me, and too soon an old man out of me. And now this highway takes me home.

I drive a good old truck. I call her Jesse, after Governor Ventura's raid on the treasury sent every Minnesota man, woman and child a government check in the mail. I snatched her off a lot in Pelican Rapids. She wasn't much to look at, all floppy and forlorn, a drippage of oil beneath her and North Dakota State University still on her doors. But she had new belts and hoses and good rubber. She rattles a bit going uphill, but she never runs hot pulling a load.

And she pulls a load today, me and Miss Judi, sundry

household goods, a 200-pound Newfoundland dog, and behind it all, a homemade trailer filled with what little I own.

I want to tell you about how the years and the women whittled me down to nothing, about Miss Judi, long and lovely and freckled in places you'd blush to believe, but with a chainsaw deep in her soul that over-revved on moonlight and whiskey. But I will tell you instead about how another hill got between me and Alaska. I was Fairbanks-bound when there was a hellfire of smoke and a crack like the devil's bullwhip and I was standing alongside Highway 61 with a broken crankshaft and cold weather coming on.

I cobbled the truck back together while I waited on spring. First on a mildewed mattress in a basement in Saint Paul, not far from where F. Scott Fitzgerald sipped too much whiskey, then to a careening row house near the foot of the old Mississippi High Bridge, groaning nights like some great tortured beast. Then there was a farm along the Otter Trail, where the lakes glisten and the waters flow to the great Arctic Sea.

Land went begging in those days. Taxes were a dollar an acre, long-neck Buckhorns three bucks a case. The marijuana grew higher than the corn and the women were intent on fulfilling the Lord's command to Noah to go forth and multiply. There was the flash of maple each fall, roiling woodsmoke and thundering ice wintertimes and the riot of long-overdue springs, summers with sweet horses nickering along the pasture fence.

But that's all a dream now, thirty years like a skein of southbound geese. The road drops to the river and the trees rise to meet us, while I careen downhill in a truck old enough to vote.

Oh Minnesota, the things you taught me, hard lessons of life and love. To sneak on a buck and to kill him cleanly when he bolts from his bed. To whipsaw a dogsled through deep timber. To know when sap becomes syrup, when to plant and when to reap, the lilt of Ojibwe, the clatter of Finn, the smells of each of my children, wet and wriggling and newborn in my arms. Slush and mud and dust and mosquitoes, each in its own season. And always the rocks and stumps and gumbo clay and machinery that tried to bite me.

And now I am coming up fast on Wisconsin. I will make it but Miss Judi will not, and I will have bittersweet memories and a Newfoundland dog who will never quite understand why he cannot lap the ocean like lake water.

I do not know that just yet. But I know I will be ready with a heart forged with fire and ice. Now the old truck rattles and hums while the Minnesota hills drop forever away.

Of Time and River

The Old Man was in fine form that afternoon. Engaged in direct conversation, he would look me square in the eye, fix me with the ferocity of an osprey. But when the spirit started working and a story came boiling up, he would look off at the horizon, almost like he was reading a script off the sky.

The Old Man wore two hats. He was Capum Roger, master of the *Sweet Bedelia*, a workboat building docks, bridges, and seawalls from Daufuskie to Whale Branch. And he was also The Honorable Roger Pinckney X, Beaufort County Coroner, the only man vested with constitutional authority to arrest the sheriff. The unlikely conjunction of those two occupations made fertile ground for an extraordinary blooming of the Southern Oral Tradition. But I was only ten at the time, way too young to know everybody's daddy couldn't talk like that.

It was late spring, 1956. I was sitting on a stump on the edge of a piney bluff, looking out at the fine green marsh, soaking up another one of the Old Man's tales. Beyond the waving marsh and wrinkling blue water, the golden stripe of a sandbar was shimmering in the afternoon sun, level with the water, blonde and beautiful, like the hair of a woman swimming against the tide. There on the west end of the bar, square as a shoebox and dark with oysters and barnacles and seaweed, lay an encrusted firebox and boiler, all that was left of the *Clifton*.

The *Clifton*. That was why I was there on that stump, so long, long ago. The Old Man had taken me in tow for the day, and, as always, had solicited my good behavior with a bribe. If I would wear my hat, take it off indoors, speak respectfully to my elders, not beg incessantly for Moon Pies, Nabs, or Dixie Cola, he would grant me a special request. And my request was always the same. We would go sit in the woods, look out at the river, and he would—once again—tell me how the *Clifton* came to grief.

But it was more than that. Far more. I got a rare hour of his undivided attention. And it was an invocation of times I had never known. Days of my father's father, gone three weeks before I was born. Days when shuffling and diminished legions marched each Confederate Memorial Day, when the Gullah celebrated separately, dumping extravagant garlands into the gurgling ebbtide in grateful remembrance of the Yankee sailors who had set them free. Times when there were no highway bridges to my island home, when the *Charleston and Western Carolina* huffed down from Augusta, dropping passengers at Yemassee and Pocotaligo, Beaufort, and, finally, Port Royal. When the *Pilot Boy*, *Clivedon*, *Katie*, and *Clifton* wound their way up from Savannah, hauling mail, passengers, and freight to Daufuskie, Hilton Head, Bluffton, and Parris Island. When the long, low wheeze of a steam whistle sent every living soul to the Bay Street docks to gawk and speculate about persons and cargo coming ashore. Where stevedore Jim Bledsoe once fell overboard, with an anvil under each arm, then came thrashing and cursing to the surface. "If one of you bastards don't help me with these anvils, I'm going to let one of them go."

Katie burst her boilers, catapulting the unfortunate engineer high into the air and down the belching smokestack. *Clivedon* went in for inspection, never came out, was cut up for scrap. So did *Pilot Boy*. Collectors are still wondering what happened to the fine carved eagle that adorned the wheel house. And the *Clifton*, loaded to the gunnels with potatoes from Lady's Island, came to ruin off Pigeon Point.

The Old Man was still squinting at the sky, telling me about the potatoes—*Irish potatoes*, he called them, as opposed to real potatoes, which in his world were orange and sweet. The wind had come up and the tide began to fall and waves rolled up to four feet, then five, and six. The first mate advised waiting for better weather, but the captain disagreed. "I'm master of this ship," the Old Man said in a deep and affected baritone. "Cast off and head for Port Royal!"

On the Old Man's lips, it was a heroic order worthy of Columbus, of Balboa. I was spellbound, the Old Man shifting into overdrive. He held his hands out before him, palms down, conjuring up images from those days long gone.

"...and the wind and tide caught her and swung her onto the bar and set her down hard onto the sand and...*smack!*" the Old Man slapped his hands together to mimic breaking of beams and planks.

I knew it was coming, but nearly fell off the stump anyway.

"...and the who-o-o-le river," he drew his words out deliciously, "was full of Irish potatoes!"

And for an instant I could see it all in exaggerated detail—the Beaufort River, filled from bank to bank with a great raft of bobbing and rolling spuds. And I imagined little black boys and little white boys like myself running down to the riverbank from here to Land's End, scooping up buckets and baskets and bringing them home for their mamas to cook for supper. It became, in my young mind, no less a miracle than manna falling from heaven and feeding the Children of Israel.

I grew up and the Old Man grew older. In time, I went looking for my own story of the *Clifton*, something I could pass on to my own children. I found it in the May 20, 1909 issue of the *Beaufort Gazette*. The *Gazette* tells the story, a bit less fanciful, and certainly not nearly as well: "While returning from the plantation of Messrs Blitch on Cuthburt's Point Tuesday night, the steamer *Clifton* with a cargo of potatoes was caught in the severe wind and rain storm and run aground just off Pigeon Point, where now she lies, badly battered and half full of water. The boat left the wharf about half after nine with the intention of running as far as Beaufort and tying up for the night, but found the weather so rough and the night so black that she decided to anchor in the creek. After spending some time there, the tide commenced to turn, and as the creek was very narrow at that point, it was feared that if she remained she would be battered against the banks so the anchor was heaved and the trip continued until she struck the bank at about eleven o'clock and commenced to fill. The crew was set to work at the pumps but this was found useless...."

Captain George Beach, the *Clifton*'s owner, arrived from Savannah aboard the *Pilot Boy*, surveyed the damage, and proclaimed his ship a total loss. The sidewheeler *Thetis* came up from Port Royal and salvaged what potatoes it could. A week later the wreck "proved the center of attraction for Beaufort folks," according to the *Gazette*. "Row boats, launches, tugs, sailboats, and steamers have all taken their share of the curious to visit her." Jerry Potter of Beaufort bought the wreck and dismantled it to the waterline. The pilot house went to the Point, where it was used as a bathhouse for those swimming in the Beaufort River.

I never told the Old Man about the article I found in the *Gazette*. There was nothing in it he needed, nothing to improve upon that treasured staple of my childhood. But one day, when I was past fifty and the Old Man pushing ninety, another *Gazette* article caught his eye. A southbound yacht had encountered the remains of the *Clifton*, and limped into Beaufort for repairs. The *Gazette* had incorrectly identified the *Clifton* as "a Civil War wreck."

First, any reference to that long-ago conflict as a "civil war" was bound to arouse his ire. Only Yankees call it that—and Beaufort is full of Yankees these days. It's the *Wa-uh Between the States*. So the Old Man had written a letter to the editor, politely ignoring the great *faux pas* of calling so epic a struggle by the wrong name, but taking him to task about the misidentification of a lump of rusted iron and marine growth. The paper subsequently printed a correction, the Old Man proudly related.

And then he looked off into the middle distance again and I wished I had an oak stump to sit on. But the stump was gone, and the piney woods were gone to houses. All that was left was the river and the wreck of the *Clifton* and the Old Man and a boy who was a boy no longer.

"I was out on the river in the *Sweet Bedelia*, fishing on the rising tide." His voice was raspy and the Camel straights he smoked years ago were still fluttering way back in his throat. "All of a sudden this big Yankee yacht comes around the bend and runs right into the *Clifton*. He wallowed around awhile, and I came alongside and asked him if he needed a tow."

There was a long pause. The Old Man blinked and his eyes watered, almost like the stretch of years were too great for tongue or remembrance. "I gave him a line but told him not to start his engine, just steer on our way down to Beaufort. Well, after a mile or so, there was a big blast of smoke from his stack, and he started to come around me." There was another pause, while he waited for the full impact of such idiocy to sink in. "He snatched the *Sweet Bedelia*, liked to tore the cleat out of her stern. I cut the line loose and let him take it. My line!"

I could almost see it. The white yacht boring down the river, throwing a wake high enough to swamp a bateau, the Old Man's line twirling and whipping in the propwash.

"I found him at the dock, tried to get my line back, but he was drunk, wouldn't let me have it!"

A drunk Yankee skipper at the wheel of a big yacht. Hardly unheard of, those days or these. Out on the river, there was a throb and a rumble from a towboat diesel, and the blast of an air horn came rolling along the breeze. Way across town, I heard warning bells jangle on the bridge. The Old Man's ears weren't so good anymore. Maybe he didn't hear the diesel, the bells. But he heard the horn. He cocked his head, looked out over the houses between us and blue water. "You remember the time the *Rolletta* hit the bridge?"

I remembered the *Rolletta*, lit up like a carnival, bulling ten thousand tons of slash pine down to the mill at Savannah. I remembered lying in bed a half-hour later, hearing the thunder-crack of splintering timbers. But I didn't care about the *Rolletta*. "The *Clifton*," I said, gently trying to steer him back on course.

There was a instant of confusion in his eyes. "Yeah, yeah,"

he said, like I had roused him from a deep sleep. There was another pause, then he told me how he called the Coast Guard, and the Coast Guard called the yacht's owner, who fired the skipper and sent a sober one down from New York.

I thought the tale had dwindled to nothing, but the Old Man was still looking off at the sky. "Willie Morrall was under-taker in those days. I ran into Willie and he was carrying a pistol. I asked him why. He said some sum-bitch came into his office and threatened to kill him."

Willie Morrall packing a pistol seemed a long way from a river full of potatoes. But they had the *Clifton* in common. The Old Man went on, a hint of a smile playing around the edges of his mouth. "That skipper wandered up and down Bay Street, drunk as hell, looking for the man who took care of dead people. Somebody sent him to Willie Morrall!"

The towboat blew all clear. The bells on the bridge jangled again. And a breeze came ghosting up from the river.

Guiding Light

I knew about Papy Burn long before I sat in his kitchen and drank his scuppernong wine. It was 1956 and my daddy, Capum Roger Pinckney X, riverman and dockbuilder, was writing an estimate to repair the county wharf on the New River. The deck was splintered and the piling underneath eaten clean off by the shipworms.

The Capum sent me beneath with his Boker Tree brand jackknife to probe the timbers. I bogged and hollered about soggy wood and he scribbled and figured as the tide dropped to dead low and the gnats started in on us. I came up muddy and gnawed and hungry. The boat was ready and the tide was right and there was a sandwich waiting somewhere on the other side of the river, but the Capum said, "We can't leave Daufuskie without stopping to see Papy Burn."

That was island etiquette in those days. No cell phones, no phones at all, no polite beg-offs. If we did not see Papy, he would find out we had been on the island and there would be hell to pay next time. So we climbed aboard a wheezy Dodge flatbed and wallowed down rutted roads that snaked through the timber like long green tunnels until we came to Papy's door. There was a sign on the gatepost. "Private Property, Will Shoot." And I knew enough about Papy Burn to know he meant it.

He wasn't much to look at, skinny and wizened and wild about the eyes. But Papy Burn was a legend and my personal hero. He was the retired keeper of the Bloody Point lighthouse, who had waxed poetic when he met the governor in 1952. "Governor," he said when he shook his hand, "I wouldn't trade a teaspoon of my island for your whole state!"

Noble sentiments. I loved Daufuskie, too, and those words would carry me far—to half a dozen books and a screenplay, but also in a direction I did not particularly want—to Federal court, where I pleaded—and lost—a case to stop a highrise condo, not half a mile from where I drank his wine in 1956.

But here I am in 2002 and the cranes lift concrete onto the fourth floor while I remember how it was when I was a boy. How I fretted while Papy talked nonstop and hopped around like a one-legged fish crow and tipped a demijohn full of wine as yellow as a tornado sky. The concoction glooped into juice glasses, the bubbles stirring dubious sediment in the backflow. Papy turned to the Capum. "Now Roger Pinckney, don't you tell me this boy is too young to drink my wine!"

I was ten at the time, but Momma wasn't along and Daddy didn't say anything, so I drank all of it. Forty-odd years later, I am pleased to tell you that Papy Burn was the first of many men to get me drunk.

I was honored.

Daufuskie Island has a way of growing on you, like Papy Burn's wine. Pretty soon, if the chiggers and the skeeters and snakes and gators don't run you, or the isolation and loneliness and inconvenience drive you crazy, you won't be happy anywhere else. Papy Burn would row and sail to town for supplies, a trip he always dreaded. "I spent a whole month in

Savannah today," he'd crow upon his return.

Papy Burn—officially Arthur Ashley Burn, Jr.—came to Daufuskie as assistant lighthouse keeper in 1913. There were two lighthouses on Daufuskie in those days: the Haig Point Light on the north end, guiding river traffic across the shifting shoals of Calibogue, and on the south, the Bloody Point Light bringing ships into Savannah. Both were what mariners call "range lights." Rather than the beacon rotating like the soap opera intro, each station showed two lights. Rivermen and blue water sailors found safe passage by lining them up like sights on a rifle.

At Bloody Point, the front light shone through an upstairs dormer window on the keeper's house. The rear—a kerosene-powered locomotive headlamp—was on a ninety-foot steel tower a half-mile back in the woods. To spare the keeper the hazard of the climb, the lamp was mounted on a track and pulleys, and was lowered each morning for polishing, trimming and filling, then lit and hoisted aloft every evening, rain, fog, sleet or gale. There was a brick lamphouse at the foot of the tower, stocked with parts, tools, and spare lamps. An oil house a few yards away held drums of kerosene. House, land, tower and outbuildings cost the government thirteen thousand 1883 dollars.

The tower was prefabricated by Cooper Manufacturing, Mt. Vernon, Ohio, shipped to Savannah by rail, then barged onto the island. The shop superintendent, one J. C. Doyle, came along to supervise the work. Doyle liked Daufuskie enough to stay, going from private employment to the United States Lighthouse Service at a salary of $620 a year.

Doyle resigned in 1890 and was replaced by Robert

Sisson. Sisson weathered the Storm of '93, which sent a twenty-foot tidal surge roaring across Daufuskie. Sisson lost his horse, his laying hens, his canned beef, tobacco, kitchen furniture, pots and pans, bacon, lard, and even his shoes in that great miracle of wind. He also nearly lost his home when the surf undermined the keeper's cottage. After the wind died down, the house was jacked up and rolled a half mile back into the pines, and its dormer light was replaced by another tower built on the beach.

Sisson was transferred and his son took his place. Assistant keepers came and went and pretty soon there was Arthur Ashley Burn, Jr. Papy was well connected, running weather dispatches to ships out in Charleston harbor. He knew the deckhands and skippers and pilots and customs agents. He applied and was accepted. The government gave him $540 per year, bounced him from Daufuskie to Savannah and Tybee. By 1918, he was back as boss, no longer assistant. Papy resigned in 1923 and went to work on the government dredge maintaining the Savannah ship channel. But by then, the Bloody Point Light was history.

Up and down the coast, the government was closing lighthouses—Charleston, Hunting Island, and Tybee. Electric batteries were replacing kerosene, and the lights would turn on each night and off each morning by themselves—no cleaning, no fueling, no trimming of wicks. Automated offshore towers now marked the Savannah channel. The house and land were sold as government surplus, the tower cut up for scrap.

But Papy Burn did not forget Daufuskie. When the lighthouse keeper's cottage came up for sale again in 1926, Papy bought it and came home. Other than a wartime job in a

Savannah shipyard and his last months in a Charleston veterans' home, Papy Burn would remain on the island for the rest of his days.

He farmed, he fished, he shrimped, he was elected magistrate. He told stories and was the subject of many more. He had four wives and outlived three of them. But today, most old-timers on Daufuskie remember Papy Burn for his wine, wine that set me reeling that afternoon in 1956.

Papy Burn was a Baptist, though hardly rockribbed. He studied the Good Book, preached a few sermons, taught Sunday school, and dispensed the law with Old Testament authority. The story of Jesus' first miracle must have stuck with him. There was fruit on Daufuskie, plums and pears and grapes of several persuasions, left over from when the boll weevil got the cotton and island farmers switched to produce for the Savannah City Market.

In 1953, Papy began turning fruit into spirits at the Silver Dew Winery, setting juice a-fermenting in the lamp and oil houses. But then the government got wind of it. Daufuskie, long a haven for bootleg 'shine, was under official scrutiny. The revenuers would ride the Savannah boat, and the whistle would blow a code when the boat was still far out in the river, and there would be a great stampede up the bank, as every living soul would bolt to cover up their stills and nobody would even be left on the dock to pick up the mail. By and by the revenuers came calling and told Papy Burn he could not sell his wine any more. Papy Burn liked to brew and he liked his neighbors to stop by and drink it, so he gave it away instead.

And that's when I came in, ten years old, soaking up his wine and stories. I grew up and moved away, and one day in

1968 there was a cassette in my mailbox. Papy Burn had crossed his last river. The Capum had gone to the funeral and caught the Gullah sisters singing as they put him in the ground at the Mary Dunn Cemetery, not a mile from where he spent his best years.

The lighthouse was sold, then sold again, and became a clubhouse for the new Bloody Point golf course, and discourteous players scarred the heart pine floor with their cleated shoes. Eventually, the property was bought by a man from Pittsburgh who calls himself Lowcountry Joe in order to sell Daufuskie real estate.

But Lowcountry Joe has fallen under the spell of Daufuskie just like I did in 1956, and like Papy Burn did back in 1913. He dug into the history of the place, began wearing a lighthouse keeper's hat, dreams of replacing the long-lost tower, and—some say—occasionally sees a wizened old man sitting in a porch rocker, staring out at the golf course that used to be deep pine woods.

Does Papy Burn still live at the Bloody Point Light? Those who knew him swear he would not rest easy any place else. And me? Well, I don't rest too easy these days. And I still want another shot of Papy Burn's scuppernong wine.

Blue Root Real Estate

I want to tell you about Daufuskie Island, about the wind and the woods and the bugs and the snakes and the real estate tycoons and the descendants of slaves and the voodoo drums.

I want to tell you all of it, to lay it in your heart, an offering—as the Good Book says—worthy unto the Lord. But I am just a man and sometimes I cry like an osprey in the high and heaving air; sometimes I snort like a porpoise in a dead-end creek and the words just won't come.

But I slept on the beach last night and saw the new moon over the dunes at sunrise, a crescent coasting above a casual slurry of pink and blue, like God got up late and slung color over his shoulder before stumbling off to make coffee.

Plovers and sanderlings skittered up and down the backwash, and shrimp boats were working Grenadier Shoals. Way offshore, the sea buoys flashed red and white and faithful, while the sunlight gathered and the colors faded and the moon disappeared into a great glory of morning.

And all the while the surf was whispering, *shawoosh, shawoosh*, secrets only those who love this place can hear. Let me tell you what it said.

Daufuskie. It gathers in the back of your throat and rolls off your tongue like poetry. *Daufuskie*, sharp like a feather in Muskegon, the Old Tongue, from the arrowshaft sandspit jutting out towards Savannah. Pat Conroy wrote about it and Jimmy Buffett sang about it, this southernmost island in South Carolina. Three by five miles, timbered, green, and forever bridgeless, forty-five minutes by boat from Hilton Head and a world away from anything you ever thought was real.

The Indians lived here for ten thousand years. The litter of their campsites, the shells, the shards, their stone-age tools, lies scarcely covered by last year's leaves. Then came the white man and his cotton and the slaves he brought from the Gola region of West Africa. The slaves toiled here for one hundred and fifty years and took this place to their hearts. When the Yankees set them free, they stayed, taking up farming and fishing and oystering. But pollution killed the oysters and stunted the crabs and drove the self-sufficient rivermen from the island. The pines overran the fields and the shanties stand forlorn, careening, and forever empty. Wild turkeys skitter through a great riot of azalea and camellia, and the diminutive island deer ghost through thickets where once grew collards and peas and okra. A few Gullah still hang on, but only two dozen where there used to be two hundred.

There are 45,000 people on Hilton Head and upwards of a quarter-million in Savannah, and you can see both places from Daufuskie. Little wonder developers want Daufuskie for golf, tennis, condos, and gated communities—plantations, they call them—where you can't go unless you belong. Little wonder they covet these miles of rolling surf, these ancient brooding oaks, this land passed down among the Gullah, our last and best link to West Africa. Twenty years ago, developers came like Pharaoh's host in the old Gullah spiritual, two hundred million dollars strong. But the waters came together and Gucci shoes wouldn't save them and they went down in a Red Sea of ink—International Paper, Halliburton Oil, and Club Corp, among a great drowning of lesser corporations.

Some say marine transportation did them in. Daufuskie is damned inconvenient. Every screw, every nail, every golf ball, T-bone, jug of whiskey, employee and customer has to be hauled across Calibogue Sound, deep and wide and dangerous as a two-hearted woman. And then the garbage and customers and employees and money must be hauled back.

It's four-dollar beer and four-hundred-dollar hotel rooms on this side of the river, and if you think you like it well enough to stay, a thousand-square-foot cottage may set you back half a million bucks. Cell phones don't work here and the internet is slower than a pelican flapping upwind. There is no ATM, no yoga and no yogurt, and after six or seven months, your woman will get island fever and likely give you trouble.

You can call it voodoo, you can call it hoodoo, or you can call it conjuration or maybe rootwork like the anthropologists do. But the Gullah don't call it anything at all. Like the Name of God to the Children of Israel, this ancient magic is too fearsome for utterance. There may be upwards of a thousand conjure doctors scattered from Jacksonville to Cape Fear: sisters Miriam, Marguerite and Magdalene; mothers Kent and Katrina; doctors Snake, Crow, Fly and Bug.

But the greatest among these is Dr. Buzzard. From African-born slave patriarch to his great-great-grandson, a Dr. Buzzard has been working here since before anybody remembers. Ax-cut or snakebit, lovesick, took sick, or trouble with the law, Dr. Buzzard is your man. That gal won't give you none? Get some

Essence of Bend Over and you'll have more loving than you can handle. Got a man pestering you? The Blue Root will make his chickens quit laying and his cows and well dry up and pretty soon his head will turn around backwards and he'll walk down the street barking like a dog.

The trouble started back in 1984 when Melrose Plantation set a real estate office on a slave graveyard. Locals called in the NAACP and the Cristic Institute. Papers flew and witnesses were deposed and a court date set while *60 Minutes* philosophized disgrace. But then a flock of buzzards took roost around the ferry landing, and Melrose moved the office and then so quickly went broke there was not even money to pay the housemover.

Melrose property owners picked up the pieces and tried to put them back together while the fairways grew weeds and the boats grew barnacles and the hungry sea began nibbling at the beachfront inn and at the eighteenth green of their Jack Nicklaus-designed course. Melrose was just about whittled down to nothing when Club Corp of America stepped in with a five-year plan to make Melrose public and turn Daufuskie around. CCA pumped six million cubic yards of sand upon the eroding beach at about a buck a yard, a project that drowned five men. They remodeled the inn and thirty-six rental cottages, bought boats, buses, mowers and trucks, and dropped another six million into a center for corporate gatherings. But then came September 11 and CCA laid off two hundred, cancelled six thousand reservations and began hauling their best equipment away.

On Haig Point, the most gated of gated communities, the story was much the same. International Paper bought twelve hundred acres on the north end of the island in 1984, carved twenty-seven holes of golf out of the maritime forest, drained swamps, filled wetlands, and offered seven hundred lots at up to a million dollars each. Haig Point did not bankrupt International Paper, but it cost them eight hundred-odd thousand dollars every quarter for twenty years. Eventually, this carnage got too much and International Paper turned the facilities over to the property owners—but not the unsold real estate. This provoked a flurry of litigation and a ruthless increase in annual assessments, ten percent per annum, *compounded*, which threatened to drive the less affluent from their property.

Down on Daufuskie's south end, Bloody Point never had a chance. Named for an old Indian battleground, Bloody Point's developers were sued by local Gullah when they attempted to block access to another cemetery, and then by a coalition of their own investors claiming interstate fraud under the same statutes that put Panamanian dictator Manuel Noriega in jail for life. There is a deserted golf course, a clubhouse, empty employee apartments, one hundred and ten lots and only seven houses, three in imminent danger of falling into the sea.

There are two large undisturbed tracts remaining on Daufuskie, former cotton plantations Webb and Oak Ridge, twelve hundred acres total, a glorious green stripe from tidal river to the sea. The land has been bought and sold and optioned and abandoned by a long and confusing line of corporations, all beset with unexpected financial woe. Developers call these tracts the key to Daufuskie's future, but for some reason, the key won't quite fit the lock. Today, the very last of the oceanfront real estate on the east coast goes begging, and you can take a nap on any of three golf courses and a gator might wake you, but not likely a golfer.

I came by this naturally, heir to this great gumbo of history, culture and magic. I was born to it, the eleventh consecutive first son to bear my name. My people fought the Revolution, signed the Constitution, served the Confederacy. It took three generations to recover from General Sherman, but by the time I came along, my daddy, Capum Roger Pinckney X, was making a pretty good living, building docks and seawalls and hauling freight over to Daufuskie on his workboat, the *Sweet Bedelia*. I rode along whenever I could, and roamed the woods, bogged the creeks, climbed the trees, and swung from the vines. And I fell in love with this place, its eccentric and fiercely independent people, the deep brooding woods, the surf now thundering, now whispering, falling, falling upon a beach like a broad band of polished copper.

Daddy was also county coroner, a doctor to the dead. Called out at all hours for drownings, knifings, shootings and car wrecks, Daddy would take pictures and make notes and call up a jury to decide who to throw in jail. But scattered throughout thirty-six years of accidents and mayhem came what Daddy grinned and called "death by undetermined natural causes." It was a code that everybody—from the sheriff to the judge to the undertaker—knew: Dr. Buzzard or one of his colleagues had been at work.

I got the dark from Daddy and the light from his Gullah deckhands, Horace Brisbane, Dan Williams and Cuffey Dawes, but mostly from Miss Elvira Mike, mammy to my father, my uncles, my cousins, and finally, me. I figured her a confidant of

Methuselah and knew she was at least old enough to have remembered the battleship *Maine* taking on its last load of coal at the Port Royal Naval Station on its way to Havana and destiny in 1898.

Elvira sat me upon her knee and spun up a world long gone, a world of cotton and rice and slaves, the stories and spirituals and field hollers. When the spirit got to working, she would leap from her chair and do a ring shout right there in my grandmomma's kitchen, heel and toe, round and round, clapping beats and half beats, in a dance of praise going all the way back to the west coast of Africa, before the slavers threw her great-grandmother into chains. I clapped and jigged along as best I could and by the time I was twenty and moved up north, I was so black nobody would rent me an apartment over the phone.

In 1998, I wrote *Blue Roots*, a primer to Gullah folk magic, about the hants and hags and jack-mulaters, the hexes, spells, and conjure doctors, but especially Dr. Buzzard. I knew the old Gullah were passing and I figured to set it all down—historic preservation, not bricks and mortar, but breath and flesh and bone—before it was gone.

Fool me. I came back to Daufuskie a year later and found all of it very much alive. I met Miss Emma, who cooked fried chicken that makes a man want to rush out and buy Melrose real estate—or used to, before Dr. Buzzard took over. I met Capum Bud, who lost his truck, his job, and finally his health after he threw a Gullah stowaway off a Melrose ferry and got a voodoo doll in the mail. I met Clarence, *born wif de caul*, the amniotic sack over his eyes, who sees so many ghosts they have become *as natchel as a man wif britches*. I went over to

Savannah and met Angel, who can look in your face and tell you more than you want to know about yourself, who can call up money and love and make rich white women weep and tear their hair and run all over town spending money. I met Bloody Mary, who gave me a High John the Conqueror, the king of the root world, after the developers threatened to run me off for meddling in their business.

You can blame that on Miss Sally. Miss Sally and I are cousins a couple of times over, and I wasn't back on the island two weeks when she showed up at my door asking my help to defeat plans to dredge a fifty-acre boat basin into the heart of the island. So eight of us met on a shrimp boat and put our names to paper and raised Dixie cups full of good champagne and toasted, "To the woods!"

We called the State and we called the Feds, and told them about the ancient Indian camps and pretty soon we had the developers so tangled up it would take them years to cut through the snarl.

It was the first time white folks had challenged the developers and all hell broke loose. They sank one of our skiffs, threatened to burn Miss Sally out, blackballed a gal I was sweet on at the time, got me fired from a job before I ever got to work at it. But when they started talking of throwing a bag of reefer under my porch and calling the cops, I called Angel.

"Angel, Angel!"

"Wha's wrong, chile?"

I shifted into Gullah. It rolled on my tongue like a salty oyster and Lordy, it tasted good. "They be a man pester we."

"Uh-uh." I could almost see her shaking her head. "Write down he name," she said, "and make shore you spell um right."

I did and ran into her a couple of months later. "That man still pester you?"

"No, he have heart attack and done been lay up in hospital." Angel smiled. "How bout dat?"

And then there was the five-story condo planned for the front beach, thirty-six units, seventy-eight feet tall, one hundred and fifty feet from a beach that was washing a dozen feet each year. We called the State like we did with the boat basin, we called the Feds, we went to county meetings and got articles in the local press. But nothing worked until a neighbor, deep into depression and an afternoon libation, walked out into his pecan grove and hollered at the buzzards. Two days later, the U.S. Fish and Wildlife Service came up with the first bald eagle nest on Daufuskie in fifty years, not a quarter-mile from the proposed condo site.

By the time it was over, thirty-six units had shrunk to twelve, the top floor was gone, the project was seven months behind schedule and everybody wondered just how long it would be before the bankers lowered the boom.

Strike up another for *de doctah*?

But did Dr. Buzzard really put the Blue Root on Daufuskie? Did he watch *60 Minutes* and gather lizard feet and crow feathers and graveyard dirt at midnight while the Spanish moss moved in the seawind and the palmettos rattled like Ezekiel's dry bones? Did he mutter off to his backyard office, mumble soft words in Bantu while the candlelight leapt and danced over African statuary and pictures of Jesus and John F. Kennedy and Martin Luther King? You don't dare ask.

But you can believe what you want here on Daufuskie, a world away from anything you ever thought was real.

Burying Miss Louise

Prince Rivers, the last black man on Haig Point Plantation, dropped dead when the developers told him he had to move. The Scouten brothers had left him there as a young man, after the big plantations went all to hell, after the boll weevil took the cotton and the blight took the potatoes. "Move into the big house and watch after the place," they told him. "We'll come back directly." But they never did.

The land was sold, then sold again, each time with Prince Rivers part of the deal. But Prince got old, then older, and he couldn't brush out the roadsides or clean the ditches or tighten the fence and, finally, not even cut firewood anymore. So he waited for the Scoutens and burned the porch railings to keep warm, then the decking, and finally the siding and the framing, one wall at a time until there was only a single room at the middle of the house with the old cornshuck insulation all soggy and bedraggled and the roof about to fall in and a pitiful rusting stovepipe sticking through a hole in the south wall.

That's what the house looked like when they found Prince Rivers in the garden, just after the buzzards did, face down in a riot of magnolia and azalea and camellia. They buried him in the old slave graveyard, where the graves face east so the spirits can fly home to Africa, next to his kin and to the Bryans and the Simmonses and the Champions. Next to where we will be burying Miss Louise.

Down here on Daufuskie, there are 150 of us on five thousand acres, no bridge, no bank, no traffic lights, no traffic at all. The fast food has hooves and horns and fins and feathers. There's no gas and no law, except the immutable statutes of God and time and tide.

We are Gullah, descendants of slaves. We are white, shrimpers, crabbers, potters and poets, dope runners gone out of business, and a dozen shell-shocked real estate types and the corporate retirees they brought here when it looked like this place would someday become the next Hilton Head. Lord knows the developers tried, but it never did take. Today, the trees are still standing and the bucks ghost the edges of deserted fairways and wild turkeys skitter through the oleanders at the edge of your yard.

The Gullah got land with freedom, on "The Great Day of Jubilee," as they call it. A hundred years later, you would have had to put them in chains to make them leave. But hard times and few jobs and land taxes are doing what chains didn't. The Gullah have been drifting away, nearly gone now, crossing the water to Charleston and Savannah. And those who swore they would die here are getting their wish. One by one, like Miss Louise, they are crossing the river too, crossing over Jordan.

Miss Louise Wilson was well thought of and the mourners have come from all over, by bus and car and, finally, by boat across the blue and rolling Calibogue, the estuary separating Daufuskie from South Carolina and the rest of the world. Her ancestors worked Haig Point cotton, but she grew up next door on another plantation called Cooper River. She was skinny and acidic and philosophical, her skin the color of a tarnished penny from a healthy dose of Cherokee on her momma's side. She was old and these Gullah revere their elders.

But mostly the local folk loved her for her daughter Yvonne.

Yvonne (say it E-vonne) grew up here on Daufuskie, running barefoot on these sandy roads beneath great mournful oaks and towering pines. She went to school at Mary Fields Elementary, long before Pat Conroy launched a literary career by teaching there and getting fired for insubordination. Yvonne migrated to Savannah when pollution from the paper mill killed the oysters and drove the last self-sufficient Gullah rivermen off the island.

She came back when the developers promised jobs, and she found one, driving a bus between the ferry dock and the new beachfront inn. But she also found a real estate office sitting square atop a slave graveyard.

Now you can cut the developers some slack if you wish. Road easements down here are simply paths everybody has always walked. Property lines are where your great-granddaddy strung his fence to keep the wild horses and free-roaming cattle out of your great-grandmomma's okra, peas, and corn. And titles to land, passed down without probate from slave times, keep a tribe of lawyers up at night.

You can cut them some slack if you wish. Your great-granddaddy is dead and your relatives moved to Savannah and New York and Philly, and the sad and careening shanties stand forever empty. The wild island horses—the Marsh Tackies here since the conquistadors—have been corralled and barged away. The few cows and scattered goats, sure symbols of wealth in the African tradition, are tethered to keep them off the golf courses.

The developers moved back a few dozen feet from the nearest tombstones—and excavated for their reception center anyway. But when they began unearthing bones from older unmarked graves, they just threw them into the Cooper River and kept on digging. And then, you knew you could cut them no more slack.

Yvonne Wilson cut them no slack and lost her job. She was thrown off company-run ferries and ostracized by her Gullah neighbors hoping for jobs in the new developments. But, finally, the story reached the Cristic Institute and the NAACP Legal Defense Fund, and in 1989, after a segment on *60 Minutes* provoked a flurry of national outrage, the developers agreed to move their reception center.

It was a little victory in a long war, a war that our most African of cultures is losing—losing land and language and collective memory to the Great White Hoax, to assimilation and taxes and public education and mass communication, to this great shift of history, while the live oaks weep their long strings of Spanish moss and the last of the old Gullah go to ground.

As we gather for Miss Louise's funeral in the dappling shade outside the First Union African Baptist Church, we sense both the loss and the victory. We feel it, but we do not speak it. It is in this sandy ground beneath our feet, ground that would cry out if it could. It is in our bones and in our blood and in the very air we breathe, white and Gullah alike. So we stand around and shake hands and make funeral small talk, me and the other white neighbors in the best clothes we can muster, khakis and clean denims, sport jackets, and maybe a tie scattered here and there among us. The Gullah are in all their fin-

ery, the women voluminous in white and purple and green,
wearing hats like square-riggers under full sail, the men with
their spats and gold-headed canes and suitcoats that catch the
sun like a drake mallard's head.

The hearse is a Ford pickup, Jesse Williams at the wheel.
Jesse is Yvonne's man, or used to be until she ran him off.
Yvonne has two daughters grown up and gone off the island
for work, ten-year-old twins still at home, and a young grand-
son she cares for in the Gullah family tradition. She pulls in
around three hundred dollars a week maintaining Daufuskie's
dirt roads, the only black female motor grader operator in
South Carolina. Jesse came back around when Miss Louise
died, and Yvonne—wore down to about nothing—let him in.
She sits beside him in the cab. The twins ride in back with
Miss Louise, supine in her plywood box, a twist of wild
Cherokee roses on the top just starting to wilt in the hot
September afternoon.

The pallbearers wrestle the casket inside and I follow and
sit down next to Miss Wendy. Miss Wendy is from Wisconsin,
with half a lifetime in the advertising trade. She took sick a
dozen years ago and came south for her health, first to Hilton
Head, then Daufuskie. When her doctors finished with the
chemo and the radiation she knew she would never have children of her own, so she latched onto Yvonne's twins with a
biological ferocity. This dance with death so marked her that
she can't even drive by a church without misting up; and here
in the First Union African her tears flow freely.

The preaching is Baptist—long and good, about the generations springing up and being cut down like grass. The funeral
director, the *funeralizer*, the Gullah say, has the "catchers"—his

wife and two male assistants—stationed before the casket. There are eulogies and scattered prayers and, finally, we join hands for "Amazing Grace," words from a repentant slave ship captain put to an African melody so long ago. And the music dies and there is an eternity in a single silent second, and then a great shriek of grief, a guttural howl of rage and despair, as Yvonne leaps across two pews and throws herself atop the casket.

She sends the funeralizer's wife sprawling, store-bought flower arrangements clattering to the floor. The men peel her away from the casket and haul her outside while she kicks, thrashes, and claws at the air, moaning now not only for Miss Louise, but for all the generations stretching back to her ancestors in chains, for the land lost and the water fouled, for her older children grown up and gone, and for the twins, sure to follow as Daufuskie's Gullah dwindle to memory and to names on a few scattered stones.

The whites file outside in stunned silence. The Gullah follow, nodding, satisfied that Yvonne's grief has found appropriate release. I find her in the pickup, halfway through a cigarette. "Don't know why I fell out like that," she says.

I take her hand. "You did right," I say.

Jesse climbs in behind the wheel and backs the truck to the church door and the pallbearers load up Miss Louise. The twins climb on again and this curious procession lurches to life—Yvonne's pickup first, then a smoking sedan and another pickup, followed by a long string of golf carts in various states of disrepair, and finally a derelict and groaning school bus—a long-ago gift to First Union from the Port Royal Baptist Church—wheezing and steaming, loaded to capacity, a great iridescent Gullah rainbow showing through its windows. From

School Road to Church Road to the front gate at Haig Point, where the sign says you can't go unless you belong.

But the Haig Point security guards know better than to try and stop Yvonne. She has made arrangements and Hampy has brushed out the cemetery and Clarence has dug the grave. The security guards, in this most gated of gated communities, head this parade of death and life down the avenue of oaks that used to lead to the big house where Prince Rivers waited for the Scoutens, where the camellias still grow wild in the cool green woods and the golf fairways twist through the timber and the million-dollar homes nestle in the pines.

"Ashes to ashes, dust to dust," the preacher says at the grave as he throws a handful of Daufuskie Island dirt upon the casket. There are a few more words and another hymn, and then they lower the casket into the ground. The twins throw in slippers, glasses, false teeth, and Camel Straights after it so Miss Louise will not come back looking for them. Yvonne gathers her young grandson and the funeralizer knows what's next as surely as he knew she would rush the casket. He studies the edge of the grave, the caving sandy hole with the plywood casket in the bottom, and says, "You ain't passin' that baby. Somebody gone fall in that hole and they be a lawsuit."

But Yvonne has her mother's grit. "He's my grand and I gone pass him," she says.

So she leans as far over the hole as she can without toppling in. Jesse leans from the other side and I catch him by the belt and pull so he won't fall in too. And the baby goes over the casket and now we know that Miss Louise won't come back looking for him either. We all take turns with the shovel and pretty soon Miss Louise is in the ground.

We will go home and ponder all these things. Tides will ebb and flood, the winds will blow, and storms gather out at sea. In about three days, Yvonne will run Jesse off again and he will steal a pistol and go looking for Freddy, convinced that Yvonne is seeing another man. But Freddy will not avail himself and Jesse—all primed to shoot somebody—will wind up at Yvonne's and shoot her in the head.

Yvonne will fall but not die. The twins will bolt and hide in the bushes beside the house. The fire department will ring Yvonne's house and call the sheriff and wait three hours until he arrives. But Miss Wendy will get there first and when they try to send her home, she will not go. She has beaten cancer and she fears neither bullet nor arrest. She will cross the line and gather the twins and take them to her house and feed and comfort them.

And later, Deputy Gunny Barr will talk Jesse out of his pistol and Jesse will get twelve years of hard labor, and they will strap Yvonne to a gurney and haul her to Savannah, and she will come back to Daufuskie, slurring and stumbling for the first few weeks, and then stand up at the First Union African Baptist and testify, thanking Sweet Jesus for His love and Great Gawd A'mighty for giving her such a hard, hard head.

Miss Wendy will later join the church and they will dress her in a white robe and lead her to the river. And there the deacon will pray and the preacher will pray and Yvonne will stand on the bank with the sisters and they will all clap their hands and sing:

> *Wade in the water, children,*
> *Wade in the water,*
> *God gonna trouble the water.*

And Miss Wendy will weep and they will plunge her into the ebb tide so the river will carry all her sins away. And then she will slog ashore and those who see her will not be able to tell salt tears from salt river, but they will all gather round and welcome the new white member of the First Union African Baptist Church.

But we do not know any of this yet. Briefly stuck in time, we stand by the fresh grave in a great whirlwind of history and magic and grief, as the knot of mourners drifts away in twos and threes and the security guards fidget and the Spanish moss moves in the seawind, freshening now with the changing tide. But we do know this: Miss Louise has finally come home.

True North

The wind is from the west today, warm and wet and soft, like the breath of a woman in love. It wrinkles the water, and little waves rattle their tattoo upon the bottom of our boat. Way upstream, the water catches the sun and the river shimmers like broken glass, like diamonds.

I am a long way from home, way up on the Little Churchill River, where the waters flow to the great Arctic Sea, where the last Ice Age has not quite given up. Where the permafrost is only three feet down and it snows in June and September and the northern lights crackle and flicker and pop and set the wolves to howling. Where there are more lakes than words in English and Cree, and they stretch unnamed to the horizon and beyond.

But there are a few names here and I am learning them, learning the lay of the water and the green hills beyond, the muskeg and the peat sloughs and burns and the blow-downs. Lake names like Recluse and Pasketawakamaw and Muscowetin. Names like the Assaikwatama River and its thundering rapids at Innes Taylor.

And I give names to places that have none. Canoe Bay, where the derelict cedar freighter has washed upon the beach. To the sad and careening ruins at Trading Post Point, all deep in the spruces and overgrown with bearbrush. To Graveyard

Bluff where the fever came through in 1919 and took six Cree children. To Eagle Point where the big birds grieve and wheel and scream and soar.

Eagle Point. That's where I come booming upriver in a deep hull Lund, this late July afternoon, as the blueberries ripen and the summer fades and the northern pike go on the bite. Cree guide Raymond Wavey, dark-eyed and acorn-brown, runs the motor, points with his nose the way Indians do. "*Migizoo*," he says.

An eagle hurtles from the tallest spruce, down and down like feathered lightning. It flares before us and rides the wind along the water, so close now that even above the whining twenty, we hear the *whoosh-whoosh* of the air off his wings. It stays with us a quarter mile, then peels off downwind. We watch it go.

I turn to Raymond Wavey. "Magic?" I ask. The wind whips the word from my mouth.

He nods. "Good sign."

We pick our way across a bar of stones like brown loaves, idle into a shallow and weedy bay, and Raymond says, "Fish here."

This Raymond Wavey is a man short on words. So is his cousin Sammy, in the boat a quarter-mile behind us. Conversing together, they speak the slow and measured cadence of the husky Cree tongue. When they speak to us in English, it's just the basics. "Change lures." "Move." "Shore lunch." "Trophy." When the motor breaks down or a monster pike ghosts up alongside the boat, it's a conglomerate of each, as expedience and spirit dictate.

I throw a large and gaudy spinnerbait to the edge of the

lily pads, let it fall, then pump the rod to keep it up out of the cabbage. I've got a fine rig—seven feet of graphite with a vintage Shamano and two hundred yards of braided line with a steel leader on the business end. And it's just about like radar. I feel the spinner work and the little weeds pop by, and then, halfway to the boat, the sharp knock as a pike slashes the lure sideways. I set the hook and there is a great swirl and the rod comes alive and the drag starts talking and pretty soon stinking, and Oh Lordy, what a fish!

Here I am on the Little Churchill River, a fish on one end of the line, a fool on the other.

A fool because I did not want to come.

Blame it on Little Buster and Mr. Tee. Less than a week before, we were out in the Bloody Point surf, way down on Daufuskie Island, tearing up whiting and little sharks and dosing them with Italian dressing and laying them on the grill. Then Buster stuck his rod in the holder and walked away and something took a snatch at it and before he could take ten steps, pick up the rod, and run the drag back down, he lost whatever it was and three hundred yards of thirty-test mono.

Blame it on the hog mullet we got into while casting for more bait. They ripped through the inlet on the tide change, a veritable freeway of fish, fifty feet wide and a quarter-mile long. Buster got two or three every time he threw the net. "Ain't gonna eat no bottom-feeding mullet," he said. Mr. Tee seconded the motion. "They guts look like gear lube," he said. "And I don't mean no new gear lube, either." They didn't eat them, but I did—over at Miss Susan's house—fried up crisp with yellow grits and local tomatoes and all washed down with cold Red Stripe.

And a man can always blame a woman. So I can also blame it on Miss Susan. I got her into the boat one fine low-tide afternoon and we swatted gnats and caught blackfish and fell in love and pretty soon I did not want to be ten yards from wherever she was.

"Go," Miss Susan said. "You got to."

"Go," Travers Davis said. "You got to." Travers Davis is my outfitter, with guns and gear I strive to afford, with advice that's always free. I changed the subject and we talked about sharks and then he got me back on track again and said, "Roger, you go and I'll give you a hat. Heck, I'll even give you a shirt."

He did, too, and he sold me a gorilla-luggage-handler-proof rod case at wholesale—the Starving Artist Rate, he called it, one step cheaper than the Clergyman's Discount.

But I still needed some convincing. I went over to Susan's and lit a driftwood fire and we sat and talked while the tide changed and the surf mumbled and the moon crept up the sky, round and gold as a pirate doubloon. The Little Churchill River was five thousand dangerous and wearisome miles away from this woman and this fire and this seabreeze. The sea mineral was turning the flames all blue and green and wonderful and I had just poured myself a good stiff dram of bourbon and I figured on staying right there till Jesus got back.

But when I wobbled on home in the wee hours, there was a message from the lodge via satellite telephone: Be sure to bring a rod repair kit.

I called Susan. "I'm going," I said.

Her voice was lovely and heavy with sleep. "Good," she said. "Be careful and hurry home. I'll meet your plane when you come back."

And so off I went, with a belly full of the last mullet I would have for a spell. By ferry, by truck, by train, by foot, and by plane and plane and plane, by cab and, finally, on foot again, twenty hours later, walking down the dock to a waiting seaplane in Thompson, Manitoba.

I drew the oldest pilot and the youngest plane—both the same age—bush pilot Patrick Chartier and his Venture Air 186 Cessna. "It'll be a little bumpy till we get up a ways," Patrick Chartier said. It was and it was bumpy up there, too. So we thumped and droned along, fighting a ripping headwind, thirty-five hundred feet up and two hundred miles from the Little Churchill.

Patrick Chartier played the controls like a bluegrass fiddle, flying by instinct and eye and ear, and the plane skittered in the air like a car on a rainslick road. John Jensen, sharing the aft seat with groceries and gasoline and tackle and a twenty-horse Mercury, watched the county roll on beneath us. "Good Lord," he said. "I wonder how the fish ever found this place."

John Jensen. He was the reason I was there, way up in the pot-holey air, heading north by northeast in a floatplane half as old as me. John Jensen is an artist, a master carver of fishing lures, perhaps the best in the world. His stuff starts at a hundred bucks and runs to two grand and nobody ever puts them in the water anymore. The Smithsonian wants some, but John is so far behind he can't get enough together for a decent display.

So Peter and Paul Balega, owners of the lodge on Recluse Lake, came up with a novel idea. John Jensen would lie low for a month and carve and not tell the Smithsonian about the lures he was making. Then Peter and Paul would fly us up to fish with those spendy little things and I would take pictures and write it all up. And John would get more for his lures and maybe the Balega boys could get him to whittle them a couple. The lodge would get more bookings and Manitoba would sell more licenses and I would eat fish till I dropped and get one hell of a story. It was a good idea and a done deal as soon as I could get the gumption to get up from that driftwood fire and kiss Miss Susan goodbye.

So it was John in the jumpseat and me up front and Patrick Chartier at the controls. The seat was gnawing at my hind end, so I grabbed ahold of a strut alongside the windshield and shifted my weight. "Don't do that!" Patrick barked.

"Sorry," I said. "It ain't a handle?"

"No," he said. "It just holds the plane together."

I apologized again, then leaned over and tried to make sense of the gauges. We had swung around to true north and were burning twenty gallons of fuel each hour. I couldn't see the air speed indicator. "We doing about one-eighty?" I asked.

Patrick shook his head. "I wish. With the floats and this headwind, we could almost fly backwards."

Below was a profusion of lakes with rocky, timbered islands like emeralds set in pewter. The high ground was ravaged by fire and ice. A jumble of steep gravel ridges—eskers, they call them up here—marks the retreat of the last ancient glacier. And each summer, unnumbered acres of this wilderness burn off when the sphagnum dries out and the lightning sets the very soil ablaze. The woods come back each time, from wildflowers to raspberries to aspen and finally spruce, in a cycle that may take sixty years. And then it burns again. This is a world isolated by rapids and swamp in the summers and rotten ice wintertimes—trackless, unpeopled, untrod, the absolute end of the earth.

For two hours we flew, until the sea haze from Hudson's Bay lay along the horizon like a fine gray smudge, and then there it was below us—Recluse Lake, a swollen S-shaped curve in the Little Churchill. And upon the sandy point there was a cluster of cabins and we flew low and saw two women walking to meet the plane.

It was Miss Lynn and Miss Jackie, women of different sizes. "I hope the bigger one is the cook," John Jensen said.

And she was. Miss Jackie, blonde and round and wonderful, fed us with relentless punctuality, omelets and flapjacks and sausage each morning, and suppers of steak, fresh-baked bread, salads, and homemade pies. Miss Lynn laid a steaming pot of coffee upon our doorstep every morning and turned down our covers each night. In between, both of them charmed us continuously. Other than the eating and the sleeping and the delightful conversation, there was fishing, fishing, fishing, ten hours, twelve hours each day.

But first, Paul Balega ran down the rules. This was critical habitat management, cold water where it takes twenty years to grow a big fish. It was artificial lures only, with barbless hooks. Strict size limits. We would keep the medium-sized fish, eat what we kept, and release all the others. "Catch 'em, kiss 'em, and tell 'em goodbye," he said.

"Sounds like my social life," I replied.

Now, I have trolled upon the waters of life and come up with an amazing catch—houses, land, and horses, three lovely daughters, a fine strong son, and women who have loved me, the greatest of these being Miss Susan. But I am not the world's best fisherman. Yes, I have boated fish from Kenora to Bimini, and I have fished where some men can only dream of fishing. I can hit your hat with a hula popper at thirty yards and take a hoe and rake the scales off a big drum faster than you can change your britches. But if I catch two fish, my partner will catch five. If he catches ten, I will catch six. And backlashes? Don't even let me get started on that. Old Dan Williams, Daddy's deckhand back when I was a boy, was tearing up the redfish while I was just cussing and burning up the bait, when he looked at me and said, "Boy, you ain't holdin' yo' mouf right."

Maybe I never learned, but despite these burdensome regulations, I caught fish here.

John Jensen caught fish, too. He pulled the price tag off his plainest, a six-inch lure easily worth a good day's wages, and four days later it looked like he had dragged it behind a pickup. But fish came over the side on that lure and nearly every other one we threw at them. Pike—twenty, thirty, forty-odd inches—and six- and seven-pound walleyes we never even counted. Ray and Sammy cooked us lunch each noon, kicking together piles of driftwood, kindling them with spruce moss, and frying fish and potatoes in iron pans big as hubcaps.

And then there was one final day of fishing and the float plane would be coming and it would be time to go. John Jensen back to Minnesota, back to his knives and paint and basswood. Me back to Daufuskie, back to the mullet and the sharks and the whiting and the redfish, just starting to run now in the new moon of August. Back to Miss Susan, rich in all God's graces to women.

So here we sit in this weedy bay, swinging on the scant

breeze, me leaning into yet another pike as Ray keeps one eye on a cow moose with two calves, knee-deep in the water two hundred yards down the bank. Bull moose can get mean, and cows meaner. Old momma moose—*moosa* in Cree—is eyeing us too, like she's thinking, "If I gave much more of a damn, I'd come down there and put my foot right through your boat." She could, too, and Ray doesn't let her out of his sight.

So the pike comes rattling up against the side of the boat and Ray scoops it into the net and works the hook from its bottom jaw and holds it up while I snap a picture. It's a thirty-four-incher, too big for the pan, too small for the wall even if the law would let me keep it. We laugh and Ray says something in Cree and turns it loose. I catch another, and John Jensen yet another, and then Ray looks at the sky and says "Lodge." I reel in and John reels in and we stash our lures in the tackle box.

Halfway home, Ray, the best of boatman, suddenly backs the motor down and begins daubing over the transom with the fishnet. I look for his hat, but it is still on his head.

Then Ray comes up with a dying pike. One we had released upstream has not made it. Ray wets his glove, picks the pike from the net and holds it below the surface, massaging gills and forcing it into the seabound water. The fish makes a few feeble swipes with its tail, then rolls belly to the surface. Ray nets the fish again, then idles to Eagle Point. And there on the rocks he lays the fish. "*Migizoo,*" he says again, and then something else I do not catch. Halfway up the spruce, in a nest the size of a small car, two fledgling eaglets lift their heads above the ragged rim of wood. I stand in the boat, reeling with wonder. As the light falls through the boughs of spruce and dapples the water, the wind whispers the old secrets, the water sighs, and the air crackles with a magic we know but do not understand, this magic of true north.

Lonesome Woods Like These

The road snakes up from hardwood bottomland, up through the mournful live oaks and into the pines beyond. The trees bear the scars of fire, fire to kill the brush and bring back the grass to shelter the birds. Way overhead, a redtail circles and little bolls of clouds shed fleece like the cotton in the field right down the road.

There's a battered and emphysemic jeep with ten-year-old tags and Bo Scott at the wheel. He's brown and smiling, nimble of tongue, of hand and foot. He comments on the scenery, slips the clutch and tickles the throttle and shuttles the gears. Behind is a two-wheel trailer with a rattling hitch and a suspension dear to chiropractic practitioners—a layered affair, with dogs below and hunters above. Katie and Ted, me and Miss Susan.

The pointers whine and scratch and slobber beneath us. I would whine and scratch and slobber if I could only do it justice, this stew of history and blood and tradition at a full rolling boil. This meat of Ruark and Babcock and Buckingham, these quarter-pound birds that fly forty miles an hour and never in a straight line, the years and the fortunes expended in their pursuit, the pups whelped, the powder burned, the tears, the laughter, the lies, the books.

Miss Susan's got it pretty near as bad. She's one of those

long-legged, itchy gals, skinny and blonde and not so quiet, a gal who would run at a pheasant to shorten the shot, but would break out in hives if you lashed her to a duckblind.

We met on a ferry a while back. She was coming off and I was getting on, but I asked her out anyway. "Gin makes me sin," she said, and I asked, "Well, ma'am, what rhymes with brown licker?"

Nothing did, but that didn't seem to matter. One thing led to another and here we are on a bright November morning in a wonderment of longleaf pine, here in these sandy Georgia hills, a dozen miles north of Statesboro. The jeep sneezes, the gears howl and the springs and axles rattle like a bag of iron bones. I watch her eyes and I know she's about to whine and scratch and slobber too.

The road comes up through the timber and we jounce along and the redtail cries while the woods roll by. Finally, Bo Scott pulls into the piney shade, turns and flashes an expansive gap-tooth grin. "Here we is."

He springs the dogs and I fetch the guns. I tote my pawnshop-grade L. C. Smith twelve, barrels lopped to twenty-six, cylinder and cylinder. You can see through the blueing and there are scratches on the barrels and the case hardening is just the faintest of glories. But it's stocked better than most old guns, long enough and straight enough so you won't knuckle your cheek till your jaw goes numb and shoot under every bird from now till you get too old to hunt them anymore. And after seventy-five years of hard use and indifferent care, the snick of her closing will bring tears to your eyes.

Susan's Beretta bears nary a scratch, but she's worn the gold right off the trigger. She's quick, but aggravating as Lulu

Walls in the old A. P. Carter song. She'll slouch along, the Beretta anything but ready, maybe a smoke dangling from her lips, genially ignoring polite suggestions to put out that damn cigarette and keep her shoulders square and her feet pointing in the same direction and her eye on the dogs. But when the birds flush, she'll come up dead-eye snap shooting faster than you can think, sometimes missing, sometimes connecting, but generally shooting better than me.

We work our way uphill, through scrub oak and briar tangle, through wire grass and weeping love grass, fine metaphors for our time together, through leaves like potato chips, our vests rattling with ounce-and-a-quarter number nines, our hearts keeping time as best they can.

The dogs fan out, snuffling brushpiles, thickets and tangles, circling, circling back. Bo Scott talks them along. "Get on them birds, Katie. Come on, now, Ted."

"You got a whistle?" Susan asks.

"Some folks got whistles," Bo says, easing along with the dogs. "Some got shock collars. I just hollers."

"You hunt quail?"

"No ma'am, I hunt coon."

"You go out at night with dogs?"

"Yassum. I got eighteen hounds, blueticks and Walkers, but there just ain't no money in hides no more."

"You eat them?"

"Yassum, I shore do."

We're up in the longleafs now, with a coon hunting bird-dog man and the old magic is working. The wind sighs through the pinetops, lonesome for more woods like these—mixed hardwoods and softwoods, mature timber, with young growth springing up beneath the canopy. Lonesome for bushels of cones big as cantaloupes, for squirrels and woodpeckers and jays and owls and wrens and, of course, the quail and a bobcat or two and the deer who have left their tracks pegged everywhere into firebreaks and jeep trails.

The wind sighs for the farms and the overalled and barefooted farmers, and for the ornery mules and the country stores and the one-room schoolhouses and clapboard Baptist churches, for the rough board benches in the cedar shade where you whittled and talked and drank iced tea when it was too hot to do much else, for the patchwork of tiny fields, peas and corn and milo, for a special time, long gone, when there were quail at the edge of every dooryard, and blackberry tangles where the birds bunched up in the evenings, whistling *bob-white, bob-white*, till all the covey came home.

But there are too few woods like these nowadays. You can turn loose your hounds and bust deer and hogs loose in the hardwood bottoms, and you can hunker down in a September hedgerow and shoot at doves till you drop. You can paint your face green and back up to a tupelo and rake a slate with a stick of fat lighter—*kwook, kwook, kwook*—and if the bugs don't run you, you might eat wild turkey on Easter Sunday. You can do all these things, and we do. But most of Georgia—indeed the entire South—has long ago lost its mixed high ground forest.

It's gone to shortleaf slash, pines planted like corn, harvested like corn, the stands dark and brooding and lifeless, trees so close they steal the sky, and then the ravage of the clearcuts after twenty years. There are bigger farms and fewer farmers and most of them go off to day jobs to support their farming habit and they plant every foot of field trying to make it pay and it generally does not. But through years of good crops or poor, of scant profit or great loss, there is no place left for the birds. The wind sighs and we hear its great sorrow and it makes us thankful for the places like this.

Long leaf or short, there is a serious lack of rain in these parts, so dry it's a God's wonder the dogs can find scent at all. But they do, downwind of a scrub oak thicket. Katie locks up and Ted backstands, two noses down, four flanks fluttering, two tails trembling, a living, breathing ad for Eclipse Nearly Smokeless Powder.

I catch brown moving on brown, and then a flash of white, as a cock quail scurries to thicker cover. "Got us a bird," I say.

Katie sees it, too, and Bo knows her well enough to figure she is about to break point. He checks her with a simple command, then turns to us. "Move on up y'all, come on 'round."

Somehow, the dogs know he means us, not them. So it's Susan on the right, me on the left. One step, then two, as the seconds run like blackstrap molasses.

Finally, Katie can stand no more. She takes a single step— no, only half a step—and the birds explode into flight with a thunder of wing and feather you cannot imagine if you have never heard it. Eighteen? Twenty? I cannot tell. But they are close, too close. I hear the Beretta pop twice and I swing on a bird rocketing through the timber, left to right, a shot I seldom make. Dust flies off a pine and a single feather floats to earth.

We stand there, Bo wryly amused, the dogs disgusted, me and Susan in breathless and slackjawed wonder. "There were so many of them!" she says. "You'd think at least one would fall."

"Sounds like the Iraqi School of Air Defense," I say.

"Whew," Bo Scott says, "you shore ain't afraid of that trigger."

Susan grins and breaks the Beretta. Shells *poing* over her shoulder and swish into the leaves. I pick the single empty from the ejectorless Smith and we go after the singles.

"Uh-uh," Bo says, half to himself. "Some folks jus' wave they guns around. By the time they shoot, the birds is gone."

This Bo Scott is good, real good, at handling dogs, squiring hunters, and keeping the equipment going each season for the last twenty-seven years. "Show him brain surgery twice," Mr. Wendell says, "and he could do it the third time."

That was earlier this morning, back when we gathered in the hunt yard, by the dog pens, by the machinery shed with the jeeps and trailers in a long and ready row, by the weathered bunkhouse with rocking chairs on the porch, clapboards never burdened with paint. Wendell Marsh called a huddle and went down the rules. "No low birds. Treat every gun like it's loaded and the safety is off. Treat every hunter like he's liable to blow your head clean off."

Wendell Marsh is bossman and heir to this ground. His daddy and his uncle bought it for fifteen bucks an acre back in '31, cutting timber, sawing logs, tapping pines for turpentine, and grubbing a crop out of the scant acres fit for plowing. When the farming played out, Wendell Marsh got into the quail business, enhancing habitat, rifling the coyotes and wild dogs, and putting down birds for pay by the day hunters. A couple of years and a couple of hundred thousand dollars in the hole, Wendell Marsh went private. Now, there are sixty memberships at eight grand each and another four grand for yearly fees. There's a waiting list and you can't get in unless somebody sells out or dies.

Small wonder. Two hundred grand will get you some fine shooting—a thousand birds put down each week, eighty top-notch dogs to go after them, tractors and jeeps and trailers and dogmen like Bo Scott. It's big business here and all across south Georgia. Go online and get on your favorite search engine and punch in Georgia quail and if your hard drive doesn't roll over and smoke like a fresh high-brass empty, you'll see what I mean. There are extension agents to advise you, chambers of commerce to tout the shooting, kennels, vets, hatcheries, and even Quail Unlimited to sell you seed and lend you machinery to get it into the ground. You can hunt from horseback, you can ride out to the coveys on a mule-drawn wagon, you can walk, or jounce along behind a jeep like we do. You can join a club, hunt by the day, by the half-day, or stay a weekend or a week in a farmhouse or a lodge, and many places fish bass and bream and crappies should you tire of the birds. A dozen years ago, some professor sat down to figure what it was all worth. He came up with fifty million dollars. And the number has most surely grown since then.

A Georgia quail hunt is the perfect prescription for jittery times. It's two days by car from almost anywhere and they won't x-ray your shoes when you cross the state line. You can drink the water and pronounce the food and they speak English, or at least some variation of it. No lines, no layovers, no jet lag, no skulking bands of ragged and beady-eyed guerril-las, and you won't have to dodge a riot should *el presidente* sud-denly decide to devalue the peso or raise the price of gasoline.

Wendell Marsh hosts hunters six days out of seven, October through March. "We don't hunt Sundays," he says with a sly smile. "This is the Bible Belt. Some rockrib might think hunting on the Sabbath is a sin, but not burning you out for doing it."

That passes for a joke, but Wendell Marsh is dead serious about genetics, both in dogflesh and feathers. "I found a man who had fifteen thousand birds for sale. They were big and healthy and wild. I bought them all and he has been raising birds for me ever since. When he's out of birds, I quit putting them down. This is the closest you'll ever get to the old-time wild bird hunting."

Indeed it is. And never call these turned-loose Georgia quail tame before you try to shoot them. We expect a single, but fifteen yards from the point, three birds take wing with minor thunder. This time, we do better: me one, Susan, two.

Bo Scott is all smiles. "Whew," he says to Susan, which is becoming an all-purpose expression, appropriate for good shooting and bad. Then he hollers up the dogs. "Hunt dead! Hunt dead!"

This time, only Ted answers the command. He snuffles up all three, which takes him a while, dry as it is. But after twenty minutes, the birds are in the bag.

I look for Katie, but do not see her. "We're short a dog," I say.

Bo Scott scratches his head and looks back down the hill. "I believe she's on a point." But he says it *pint*.

We work our way back down the hill, looking for that whirligig tail above the understory.

Ted finds Katie before we do, sliding in behind her, again honoring her point. We ease up and it's not the single or the double we expect, but another covey which astounds us like coveys always do. But this time the explosion of the flush does not startle us into wild shooting. Old Elsie speaks, the Beretta speaks, and another three birds fall. The dogs go after them while we laugh and argue about who shot what.

And Bo Scott heads off with the dogs again, working to find new singles, his vest now heavy with birds, swinging with his easy step. The leaves crunch underfoot and the breeze works its way through the longleafs, sighing once more for what is not, while our hearts sing for what still is.

When Sparky
Dropped His Drawers

Sparky is big around as a jukebox, and twice as tall. One night down at Freeport Marina when everybody got into their licker, they dredged up a bathroom scale and Sparky laid his head on it and it weighed fifty-five pounds. He can whip any man on Daufuskie, but only has to once or twice each year to remind folks he still can. He's as easy-going as he is large, so when the wardens pointed their fingers at him and hollered, "You! Get in the boat!" he did.

That was all down at the county dock. It was Memorial Day and the wardens were up and down the river, writing tickets so fast you'd swear their pencils would smoke and catch flame. It was the day Sparky dropped his drawers and Lisa burned her fanny. A day when Billy figured on getting his golf carts fixed for free.

Billy is a little jittery after Vietnam, but does pretty good so long as he takes his medicine and sticks to beer. He paints houses and cuts grass and does a little light mechanicing when he has a mind to. But stuff breaks over here faster than he can fix it and his yard is all up in azaleas and camellias and golf carts that almost run.

We use golf carts on Daufuskie Island. We do not have a bridge and the barge only runs two days a week. They'll bring your truck over for a couple of hundred bucks, but you can only get gas from ten to noon every other day and at two bucks a gallon, a fifty-plus miles per gallon cart looks pretty good. Never mind the rain that blows in the sides, the skeeters that whine in and out of your ears, dust to give you brown lung, and the copperheads that might reach up and try to snag you when you weave home from Mudbank Mammy's at two in the morning. Never mind the mud in wet weather and the sand in dry that would destroy even the stoutest four wheel drive three-quarter-ton double clutching posi-traction monster pickup.

So the golf carts piled up in Billy's yard, and one night he was seized with sudden inspiration. He would sponsor the First Annual Daufuskie Memorial Day Golf Cart Grand Prix. Pick any cart from the motley collection, make it run, win the race and keep the cart. Losing entries would go back to Billy. In running condition, of course.

Capum Ed and I were on the other end of the island, over at Freeport trying to get something to eat. The beer was cold, but the charcoal was, too, and the chicken oozing red and the corn not even starting to steam. So when the tepid band struck up an indifferent version of "Carolina in my Mind" and the cook smothered the feeble fire with another twenty pounds of drumsticks, we judged the situation hopeless.

"Damn," Capum Ed said, "my belly's gnawing on my backbone. What we gonna do for supper?"

Capum Ed and I grew up together, bogging the creeks, wading the surf, roaming the woods. We picked oysters and snagged spottail and shot ducks and doves and quail. But then he went his way and I went mine—he to twenty-five years in the Navy, me to court when I refused Vietnam, then to a sentence harsh as any jailtime—thirty years on a northern Minnesota farm.

We wrote a few times. I was rolling rocks, stringing fence, raising horses, cows, and babies, and keeping my eyes peeled for the FBI, who never showed but skulked around making inquiries amongst my neighbors. Capum Ed was gunnery officer on a destroyer shelling the North Vietnamese. He was an engineering officer on a battleship shelling the Syrians. He was chasing smugglers in the Caribbean. He was driving around and around Oahu, wishing the road led to Tullifinny, Yemassee or Pocotaligo, up the Edisto, down the Ashepoo, anywhere in the lowcountry, anywhere other than back upon itself in a place they call paradise. And then the letters dribbled down to nothing.

But a dozen years later there was an invitation in the mail, official stationery, bearing the postmark of the Mayport, Florida, Naval Station. "Captain M. E. Bellamy, Jr.," it read, "requests the honor of your presence...." Six weeks later, I was sitting on a folding chair on the fantail of the USS *Antrim*, a guided missile frigate, watching Capum Ed take a seagoing combat command.

He looked so much the same, tan and trim from years at sea, with those hazel eyes that could squint out things that I could not, back when we were boys trying to find the channel through the Gale Break surf. I was grayed up and bushy, full beard, long hair, wearing an L. L. Bean plaid jacket, looking, I suppose, like some displaced jackpine savage.

I shook the departing skipper's hand and then I shook Ed's and each thought I was a friend of the other. But not for long. I had something for Capum Ed—a single black-and-white photograph from 1963, the two of us hanging off the running boards of a battered Dodge truck on the beach at Pritchard's Island, a stringer of spottail bass between us.

Capum Ed looked at the picture and then he looked at me. I would like to tell you now that not only do grown men cry, but naval officers do too. But I cannot because he did not. Miss Betty and the children were there. His parents were, too, and the mighty heft of naval tradition would not allow it. But I saw water come to his eyes. "Great God Almighty!" he said. "Meet me at the officer's club in an hour."

I did. But then I went back to the farm and he to sea. This time we wrote. And by and by he retired and I sold the farm and we both came home and took to our old habits once again. And that's what we were doing on Daufuskie Island, hungry as hell with nothing to eat.

"Come on, Capum, we can drive down to Mudbank Mammy's. They got a party going and we can bum some vittles."

It was five miles away. "You're drunk," he said. "I'll be damned if I'll ride with you. Let's take my boat."

I was not drunk—not yet, anyway. But Capum Ed would never ride in a truck when he could run his boat. The tide was brimming and the sun slipping behind the Pine Island timber, and the sky over Savannah looked like General Sherman had second thoughts about not burning it when he had the chance back in '64, like he had got run out of hell and come back as a tourist and got one too many parking tickets and finally went for his matches. We were three hundred yards into Ramshorn Cut when the blue lights popped off behind us and I knew we should have driven my truck instead.

Down at Mudbank Mammy's, the party and the fire and the First Annual Daufuskie Memorial Day Golf Cart Grand

Prix were roaring. But Billy had only two entries. A Jamaican who took an Easy Go and somehow nursed it into life, and George, who filed and gapped the points on a Club Car, pulled off the muffler, wired the governor wide open, slit the intake and pulled off the seat, and sat Lisa up on the rails with a can of starter fluid and instructions to give it a little squirt for some extra power in the straightaways.

George used to preach the Gospel out in Kansas, some say, and how he blew ashore here is anybody's guess. He's long and lean and philosophical and his old pickup lays a fine trail of blue smoke and gets about ten miles to the gallon, and he could use a golf cart real bad.

Memorial Day used to be Decoration Day in these parts, when white people stayed home and great throngs of Negroes converged on Beaufort to eat watermelon, chicken and mullet, to ride the carnival and whoop and holler and dance and drink moonshine. There'd be praying and singing and a cutting or two, a pistol-whipping thrown in for good measure, and some- times gunfire, generally wide of the mark, and a brass band parade down Bay Street to the Beaufort River, where they dumped extravagant garlands into the waters in honor of Yankee sailors and marines who had run the gauntlet of Confederate fire and taken the sea islands and set them free. But along came mass transportation and mass communication and the man on the six o'clock news, and pretty soon white folks took over and the Negroes mostly stayed home and Decoration Day got to be Memorial Day, pretty much like everywhere else.

But nothing is quite like Daufuskie Island. Now the bold crossbuck of the old Confederacy snapped from a stanchion on the end of the county dock. And above the riverwind, above the lap of waves along the shore, above the snap of the flag and the raucous country-blues on the battered boombox, you could hear two carts off in the distance, revving and rattling, sounding like two pulpwood cutters in a chainsaw fight.

Sparky met us at the pierhead. "I'm sorry, I'm sorry!" he blurted. "It was all my fault!"

It was a bit of a stretch, Capum Ed's seventy-five-dollar ticket from two wardens for a flickering stern light, the admonitions about boating under the influence, the threats of a five-hundred-dollar fine for littering when he went to throw his cigarette butt overboard. They were all up in outrage and Kevlar and automatic pistols and had no sense of humor at all.

"It's my fault," Sparky said again, his considerable head wobbling in dismay. Then he told us about the battleship horn.

It had shown up on Daufuskie shortly after they closed the Charleston Navy Base. Capum Ed, who knows all about battleships and knows they never put in to Charleston, reckoned it likely came off a destroyer, one of those whoop-whoopers they blow when chasing submarines. It was made to run off eighty pounds of steam, but Sparky had it plumbed to a contractor's air compressor with a switch jacked up to two hundred pounds. "You don't want to point it at nobody," he said. "It'll x-ray you for sure. Set you to itchin' all over."

Sparky and Turbo and Bonehead Billy and the rest of the crew down at Mudbank Mammy's were working up a serious drunk, a snake-eyed, knock-kneed, fall-in-the-ditch drunk, a drunk you just can't get in a couple of hours. They had been at it since breakfast, and the sun and some smoke and maybe the Rebel flag got to working on them, too, and they just couldn't help themselves. When they saw the wardens barrel up the river and hail another boat and keelhaul the occupants, they loosed a mighty blast. And when the wardens turned to seek the source of such auditory mayhem, fourteen people turned their backsides to the river and exposed their nether regions.

It was, by all accounts, the biggest mass mooning in Daufuskie history.

The wardens, as you might expect, did not consider this funny at all. They stormed ashore and attempted a series of arrests, "You, you, you, get in the boat!"

It was like herding cats. But Sparky was agreeable, like I said, and he complied.

While it may have been the largest mass mooning in the history of Daufuskie, it was surely not the only. The year before, Miss Mullet, blonde and beautiful and sweet-as-pie sober, had jumped aboard the wardens' boat and pulled down her bikini bottoms. She had stuck her marvelously turned posterior in the wardens' faces and they had done what most men would have done when confronted with this great glory of creation. They grinned and applauded.

And Sparky got it all on film.

"Let's see some I-D," one of the wardens barked.

Sparky reached for his wallet and produced the picture: Miss Mullet, naked from the waist down, the warden's nose about a foot short of South Carolina's sodomy statute, which you might think was drafted by a tribe of Baptist preachers.

So maybe it was Sparky's fault, after all.

The crowd was drifting away from the river, ambling in twos and threes up to Mudbank Mammy's, to the finish line of the First Annual Daufuskie Memorial Day Golf Cart Grand

Prix, which somebody had scribed in the deep sand of the parking lot with his big toe.

"*A-ree, a-ree, a-ree,*" the golf carts said, and then there was only one and a dull yellow flame flickering through the trees and then the fire sirens popped off.

Our fire department down here is something to see—offices and living quarters, a gym, four bays, an ambulance, a crash truck, two pumpers, tankers and a hook-and-ladder rig. It would be the envy of a town of ten thousand. They planned it years ago when everybody thought Daufuskie would become the next Hilton Head. But it hasn't happened yet, and the firemen spend their days driving around the island, washing the dust off the trucks, disassembling, reassembling equipment, greasing and oiling it nearly to death. Three houses caught fire here last year and all of them burned slap to the ground.

There were, of course, reasons. Miss Louise threw on too much fat lighter during that last cold snap and the stove pipe lit the wall and the shanty wasn't much and didn't last long. Both of Mr. Ted's neighbors turn in early and, though you could see the fire clean over on Hilton Head, nobody saw it here. Leroy saw wires smoking at Miss Cathy's, but Leroy was heading back from sporting one of the Jamaican gals and hesitant to disclose his whereabouts with a fire call.

But the firemen are great guys and you can go there to visit or eat venison sausage or vote or get your blood pressure checked. And if you get snakebit or fall off a roof or chainsaw your leg, they'll call up Savannah and a helicopter will land in their parking lot and fly you to the hospital for three thousand bucks.

They got on this call right quick and the woods did not catch fire and burn right up to the fire station door like last year. Come next morning, we'd learn that George and the Jamaican were wheel to wheel in the final quarter when Lisa got too handy with the starter fluid and the engine backfired and caught afire and George lost control and hit a pine and Lisa's glutimus lost its tenuous grip on the seat rails and she sat flat-assed upon the flaming engine.

So the Jamaican won and got to keep his cart, and George's melted to a great and unrecognizable pool of fiberglass and aluminum, and Lisa gimped around for a week or two, easing her considerable discomfort by sitting on a pile of boat cushions in the wheezy pickup. And Billy was short two carts and the rest of them still did not run and Capum Ed and I never did get anything to eat. And Sparky? Well, the wardens caught up with him later, and extracted serious revenge. But that's another story.

That all came later. Right then, it was just me and Sparky and Capum Ed on the county dock and the flames licking, licking out in the woods and the sirens just beginning to wail.

"Damn, Sparky," I said, "let's make up some prints of Miss Mullet and laminate 'em and sell 'em for ten bucks each. We'd all have diplomatic immunity."

He said we would, but we never got around to it.

A Windy New Moon Morning

The rail flushed from the green sedge along the creek, caught the wind and sailed off to the south, right to left, a hard shot for a right-handed man. But there was no man behind the trigger. There was no woman, either. Miss Susan lolled on the bow seat, feet canted off to one side, legs crossed, eyes soaking up the glory of saltmarsh and sky, the gun anything but ready. She scrambled and took the shot anyway and the number eights tore up the water a full three feet behind the bird.

"Cuss you, woman," I said, "put out that cigarette, get your feet under you, and keep your thumb on the safety."

She cut her eyes and blew smoke in my direction. "Didn't your momma teach you to talk nice to a woman with a gun?"

"Yassum, my momma taught me to be nice to women all the time, 'cept when they miss a marsh hen." That flew about as far from the mark as those number eights. I doubt Momma could imagine a woman in a marsh hen boat.

Travers Davis, high on the flats boat's stern platform and laboring over the pole, grinned down at us. He swung the boat to go after the bird, but there was no fighting the wind. After a few hopeless swipes, he gave up and we blew on down the flats toward a broad bend in the Cooper River.

The next bird came up from beneath the boat and Susan

shot wild and cussed and passed the gun to me. "You shoot," she said. "I can't hit a bull in the butt with a board."

I shook my head. "I've seen you bust twenty clays in a row. Skip the scenery. Pay attention and stay ready and you'll be just fine."

Another hundred yards and she got her chance, another right to left. This time she made good, folding the bird at twenty yards. This was the woman I knew, who had shot birds from here to Patagonia. "Hey baby, got your gumption back?"

She nodded and grinned and broke her trim Beretta. The empty pinged out of the gun and swished past my left ear and plooped into salt water. I scooped it up and threw it into the bottom of the boat.

"Save your empties," Travers said. "Sometimes you got to throw stuff at 'em to make 'em fly." He kept to his pole, water running from his face—sweat or spray, I could not tell. He did all he could to keep the boat pointed in the way the wind would have it go.

It had all started on Momma's porch a couple of weeks before. "Don't you bring any over here," Momma said. "I cooked enough of them when you were a boy. I fixed them a dozen ways and they all tasted like the very devil."

Momma was rocking and watching the river flow, casting aspersions upon things in general, and particularly on the culinary possibilities of the marsh hen, the clapper rail, old *Rallus longirostris*. Momma made art out of being ornery, but she was real funny if you could sift through her sarcasms.

I was there for an hour or so, walking the usual fine line between being candid and provoking maternal outrage. But I was lit up anyway. After thirty-odd years of bumming, the call of blood had brought me back to where I first saw the light, back to the Carolina lowcountry. There was a new moon coming and I was going to get after the marsh hens once again.

Momma was glad to have me home, but would have been a lot happier if I had told her I was going out with chicken necks and a dip net for a mess of blue crabs instead. "You used to pole out there in your little bateau and I'd hope you'd never find any birds. But you always did."

Yes, I did. Once or twice each season, the new moon would roll the tide way up into the highmarsh, eight, sometimes nine feet, and a stiff east wind would push it even higher until just the tips of the spartina showed like a fine green fuzz on water like burnished steel.

I'd head to the flats with my Elgin five-and-a-half, cock the motor and row when the prop would finally ball up and the Elgin would go no further. Then I'd drop the oars and pick up a pole and poke the boat into taller clumps and the birds would bust out in all directions—eight, a dozen at a time. They weren't pheasants, but I didn't know a thing about Chinese cacklers in those days, and damn, they were fun.

I had my daddy's Crescent twelve, of the H. D. Folsom Arms Company—from Norwich, Connecticut, if memory serves—impossibly long barrelled and short stocked, entirely functional but so mechanically indifferent my buddies dubbed it the Crescent Wrench. I shot sometimes and poled sometimes and always had a rotation of buddies up front. Beekman had a slippery-hammered Sauer sixteen brought back from the war, a sure prescription for holing the boat and slogging for shore. There was Mike with his Sterlingworth, not quite an Ansley Fox, but it snapped shut with the same authority. Eddie had a

.410 Savage, a ubiquitous but nevertheless bastard cousin to the Sterlingworth. Jim had the finest, a twenty-bore Parker VHE, with selective ejectors and a beaver-tailed forend, which to our eternal dismay he always rubbed down with Valvoline thirty-weight against the salt water. It was the only gun in this marvelous entourage which would not close on a cigarette paper.

It was a grand tradition going back to plantation days, but I gave it up as I got older and got after mallards and scaup instead, and later quail and turkeys here in the lowcountry and then in Iowa and Minnesota. I got married and divorced enough times to know better and before I knew it, the kids were grown and scattered and I was an old man heading back to where I came from. I settled in on Daufuskie Island, killed a raghorned island buck, got to where I could call turkeys and even sling a cast net once again.

That conflab with Momma was up in Beaufort, but Daufuskie is twenty-five miles away and considerably less genteel than my home town. A week later, I was hooked over the bar at Mudbank Mammy's when Ronnie ambled up from the county dock. The shrimp were running and Ronnie had a foot tub half full of them and brought a seven-inch specimen into the bar for everybody to marvel at. It wasn't too long before the shrimp were sold and Ronnie joined me at the bar and we talked about marsh hens. "Yeah, I like 'em," Ronnie said, "but ain' nobody hunt 'em no mo'."

"Nobody?"

"Nope, nobody. But Miss Emma shore know how to cook 'em."

That wasn't surprising. Miss Emma was famous for her

fried chicken, stewed okra, and especially deviled crabs, livened up with a mix of secret spices. Years previously, Miss Emma had cooked for the Melrose Club, during an abortive attempt to turn this island into another Hilton Head, running through ten thousand pounds of breasts and thighs and Lord knows how many bushels of crabs and selling twenty million dollars' worth of real estate in the process. "They something about Miss Emma's cookin'," locals say, "that makes a man want to spend his money."

But I wasn't thinking about land or money or voodoo vittles. I was thinking of the magic of the new moon floodtide, ten thousand acres inundated, the feeder creeks and little salt guts crackling with shrimp, and the redfish in the shallows and the cedar hummocks off in the distance and the blue sky beyond and the wind singing sad songs that only those who love this place can hear. And I was thinking of the birds driven by high water into what little marsh remained and how I would bust them loose one more time like I did when I was a kid.

The old cypress-planked bateaus of my boyhood were gone, gone to shipworms and termites and rot, but I canvassed the island and scared up an aluminum punt narrow enough for the rustling spartina, wide enough so you could stand and shoot without your sorry fanny winding up in cold salt water. I found a three-horse motor that my neighbor swore would run. It didn't. I pulled the rope out of it and when I went to fix it, about twelve feet of rewind spring leapt up at me like a copperhead snake and peeled my glasses right off my head.

I picked my glasses out of the weeds, swabbed the grease from my forehead, and thanked God He didn't choose this day to make me a one-eyed wingshooter. I threw the spring and rope and bolts in a pile and found a two-horse another neighbor said ran the last time he used it. I forgot to ask him when that was. The tank and carburetor were full of scale and varnish and pre-historic gas, but I flushed it out and got it cranked and bolted it onto the stern of the punt. Then I called my buddy Travers Davis.

Travers sells fancy outdoor duds, fine double guns, fly rods, and ten-dollar cigars over on Hilton Head. "Hey, Travers," I said, "bring over a couple of your fancy small bores and let's get after some birds."

There was a long pause. "Marsh hens?"

"Yep," I said. "I got a punt drug down to the water."

"We can use my flats boat," he said.

"No man, the punt will be easier."

"OK," he said. "I'll check the tide tables." There was another pause and the rustling of paper. "Looks like we got us a nine-foot-four-incher ten-thirty Thursday morning. That work for you?"

"Perfect," I said, "I'll meet you on my dock a little after eight."

Then I called Miss Susan. "Hey, gal, let's go huntin'."

"Where?" she asked.

Miss Susan is a busy woman and lives six hours away. But I was hung up on her real bad, so I fancied to tease her awhile. "How about doves in Argentina?"

"I can't get loose," she said.

"How about quail in Mexico?"

"I can't go."

"Pheasants in North Dakota?"

Negative again.

"Well, how 'bout some marsh hens on Daufuskie?"

"Some what?"

"Marsh hens. You know, those birds that go *kek-kek* when the tide swaps directions?"

"Hmm. They any good to eat?"

"Depends on who you ask," I said.

So there we were, nursing our blessed first coffee, watching the Cooper River, waiting on Travers. It was one of those crystalline Carolina fall mornings, when the light takes on an edge and the wind bares the first tooth of winter. The moon tugged at the sea, and the tide, two hours from full flood, roared inland and the gale galled the moving water into great rolling swells that set the floating docks creaking and plunging and sent waves crashing upon the beach. A tug bulled its way upriver pushing a wall of white water. And then came a battered shrimper and a yacht heading south for the winter, and finally we saw Travers, a mile away, now cleaving waves in great foamy surges, now nearly lost in a rubble of rolling river.

We walked out to the dock, the devil wind snatching at hair, hats, and jackets. Travers made three passes, playing wind and tide and waves until he got it right. I took a line and snubbed it off. Travers staggered up onto the float and took one look at the punt and shook his head. "That thing will drown us for sure."

It seemed a reasonable presumption. I eyed the hard case in the bottom of his boat. "What'd you bring me?"

"I got a AYA sidelock twenty," he said, "and an L. C. Smith .410. But you got to promise you won't drop that one in the river."

"I don't make a habit of throwing guns overboard," I said. "What's it worth?"

"About fifteen grand."

"Oof!"

So we cut a deal. The punt would stay on the bank, the Smith in the case. Susan would shoot her Beretta, Travers would pole, and I would spot the birds, take pictures, and offer free commentary well worth the price.

So we clambered aboard and cast off and idled across the rolling river and up into a slickwater tidal creek. A quarter-mile and the creek twisted this way and that and finally played out in a confusion of riverlets and the spartina stretched off towards Georgia and beyond. We worked our way downwind through reeds not high enough to hide a sparrow, and then Travers poked the boat into the first convenient clump of higher marsh and Susan missed that first rail.

Two hours later we had run through a box of shells and had our limit of a dozen birds. Travers eyed the marsh. There was more of it showing than ten minutes before. "Tide's dropping," he said. "We'd better get out of here."

Back on the plunging float, the wind whipping and the spray flying, there was scant time for pictures. There was Travers, me and Miss Susan with guns and birds, and when a neighbor stopped by to see what we had bagged, a magic moment with the three of us in the frame. The boat was hammering against the float and snatching at the lines. "I got to get my boat off this dock while I still have one," Travers said.

We dropped the lines and held the boat until he got the motor going, and then we turned him loose.

"Lord make us truly thankful," he grinned, "for the beating

we are about to receive…"

And then he set his jaw against the wind and hit the throttle and the boat rose and rose onto a swell and he was gone.

Susan and I watched him go, then walked up to the house, soon filled with the sweet smells of fresh coffee and nitro solvent. I grabbed the phone. "Miss Emma, you eat marsh hen?"

"Lawdy, boy, I shore do. How many you got?"

"I got you a dozen."

"I ain' had none in a long time. Brang 'em on over. I swap you some devil crab."

"Now, Miss Emma," I said, "If I eat them crab, they won't make me rush out and buy a lot on Melrose?"

She cackled. "Oh, no! You happy right there on the crick."

I looked over at Susan. She had her boots off and her feet up. "Yassum, I shore am."

"Well, come get them crab."

I said OK and figured I'd give them to Momma.

Across the River
and into the Pigs

There is an old and well-tested proverb among wild hog hunters. You pick your tree before you pick your shot.

But I am here in the New River marshes, a dozen miles north of Savannah, and the nearest tree is five thousand yards away.

I cannot see those trees, but I know they are there. They lie in an exquisite green blur along the northeast, a jumble of points and islands where the lush and riotous green of the South Carolina woods meets the sky.

The pigs are a lot closer.

I can hear them as they test the air. They grunt, woof, exceed alphabetical expression.

The wild hog has done well down here in the lowcountry. Early Spanish explorers turned domestic pigs loose upon these sunny islands so the next expedition could put ashore for fresh pork. Those hogs multiplied and later got sociable with escapees from colonial plantations, and even later their bloodline was livened up by Russian stock released by highrolling Yankee sportsmen. Given habitat and casual breeding, hog genetics go backward in a hurry. Three or four quick generations and you'll have feral critters that DNA analysis finds nearly indistinguishable from wild European stock. They look more like a dog, more like a bear, more like a werewolf, than anything you'd find in a barnyard—massive front shoulders, skinny hams, long black hair, and tusks to drive an atheist to his knees.

The wild hog remains a tribute to the wisdom of Charles Darwin. From the Carolina islands, to Catalina, to Hawaii, to the big islands of the Bahamas, to far-off Madagascar, the fittest have survived. Not only have they survived, they have prospered and multiplied. They are on the increase everywhere. The only limit to the expansion of their range is in extreme northern climes where the ground freezes and prevents their rooting during winter months.

Given the opportunity, wild hogs will eat anything. Tubers, hickory nuts, farm crops, ground-nesting birds, rats, snakes, fish, fiddler crabs, even clams, which they crack and eat— shells and all—like they were so much popcorn.

The result of this wide-ranging appetite is succulent meat the color and consistency of a turkey thigh. But it has one great disadvantage. Hang your lip over a plate of barbecued wild hog, and you will be forever dissatisfied with store-bought pork.

The wild hog is the world's most underrated big game animal. Its resume would include such words as wary, tough, mean, delicious and affordable. Even in South Carolina, where a non-resident deer license will set you back $150, a wild boar hunt costs only a modest $25 non-resident fee. For locals, it's free. Kill as many as you can—or as many as you dare. There is no limit. The only season is a careful consideration of the weather. Is it cold enough to hang a hog? Cooler up a couple of sacks of ice to pack a body cavity, and you can hunt wild hogs eight months a year. And a big hog is big indeed. A full-grown boar may tip the scale at four hundred pounds, a sow at a hundred pounds less. As might be expected, most of the ones taken by sportsmen are younger, smaller, and less experienced. Like a black bear, any pig taken in a fair chase is a trophy.

But way out here in the New River marsh, fair chase is a mere figure of speech. Fair bog would be closer to the mark. The spartina is rustling, head-high and thick as doghair. I cannot see my feet, much less the pigs, and much less the assorted snakes and gators that share this marsh.

"Don't worry about snakes if you see hog sign," Gibbes McDowell said at the beginning of the morning's slog. "The pigs eat them."

He did not say anything about the gators.

Gibbes McDowell knows about trees and hogs, having literally learned at his daddy's knee. Twenty-odd years ago, Gibbes and his father, the late Robert McDowell, were on a "let's put ashore and see what we can scare up" hunt on Beaufort County's Morgan Island. Young Gibbes was carrying his bow and had visions of venison, while McDowell senior, an incorrigible duck hunter, had brought along his old Ansley Fox double twelve and a pocketful of sixes.

But Morgan Island was thick with wild hogs. The McDowells encountered a herd in an island canebrake.

Gibbes got off a shot with his recurve bow, the arrow taking a medium-sized boar right behind the shoulder. That's when pandemonium broke loose. The herd, maddened by blood scent and squealing, sought to work vengeance upon the intruders. But pigs, however fierce and crafty, have poor eyesight. Gibbes noted the wind and thought fast. Years later, the story still makes him smile.

"I whispered, 'Sit tight, Daddy. They won't see us if we don't move.'"

The elder heeded the younger's advice until a particularly aggressive sow, previously bluff-charging everything in sight, got too close for comfort. McDowell senior headed for tall timber, McDowell junior and the sow close behind.

Though Carolina grows mighty oak and pine, there was none handy in that canebrake. Father and son had to settle for a scrubby red cedar. Father made it to the top, a scant eight feet above the mud, five above the backs of the rapidly approaching hogs. Son crowded onto lower branches, his head right next to his daddy's knee.

The bow never made it at all.

"Daddy stuffed two shells into the Fox," Gibbes recalls, "and drew a bead on the lead hog. But that sow had been in a wallow and was wearing a quarter inch of dry mud. I saw the dust fly and heard the shot rattle off her side."

The sow, more annoyed than injured, set up a racket that further agitated the rest of the herd.

"They kept coming for us," Gibbes says, "but every time, Daddy would turn them with a blast from the twelve."

They kept it up until McDowell senior ran out of shells. The hogs, scalded and discouraged, retired to the swamp. The McDowells waited an hour, then gingerly climbed down. They retrieved Gibbes's boar and beat a hasty retreat.

That was a long time ago. Right now, Gibbes McDowell is off to my right, sneaking like a Seminole. Gibbes has gone from that first Morgan Island encounter to kill maybe 150 wild hogs with a recurve bow and handmade cedar arrows. Ask him why a recurve and he will tell you he doesn't need training wheels. Ask him about the .357 on his hip and he will tell you stories to make you wish you'd never come out here, never bogged in the mud with the gators and snakes and hogs.

But I am here and I hang on to my Husqvarna 6.5. It's the utterly reliable Mauser 96 action, parkerized the color of mud, securely bedded into a composite stock, stuffed with 160-grain round-nose slugs, topped with a vintage Weaver V-4.5.

The old Weaver may be variable, but the only variation I can see is me. The spirit is willing—so the Good Book says—but the flesh is weak. My flesh—fifty-plus, a tad overweight, a mite deaf in one ear, blurry out of one eye—is now knee-deep in black viscous mud.

And the pigs are grunting.

Blame it all on Gibbes McDowell. Gibbes has the reputation for bringing home the bacon—and all his body parts to boot. If he hadn't been such a damned fine hog man, I'd never have invited myself on this foray into foolishness. I'd have called it good long ago, been satisfied with the pig I shot with number-one buck out of my little double-sixteen when I was about the same age. Would've been satisfied with the one I tacked in thick cover with my Ruger .44 rifle a few years later. And with the last one Gibbes put me on—a 150-pound sow taken from the safety of a treestand.

But no. All those pigs had a severe deficiency. They had no tusks. Tusks are inedible, and there is no room for a fearsome boar head on my already crowded walls. But a pair of evilly-curving tusks would sure look good in my curio cabinet, right next to my almost Boone and Crocket black bear skull. Right next to that shot-pocked Mason decoy. Or perhaps—should the queen of my heart concur—shining solo in the middle of a living room end table. And there is certainly room for another picture—Kodacolor, framed in weathered barn wood. Me kneeling in the muck, the sawgrass all around, bespattered, gnat-gnawed, cradling the head of a long-tusker for the camera. Gibbes McDowell smiling in the background.

So here I am, perhaps closing in on one hog too many. Or maybe two or three too many.

But the Lord looks out for drunks and fools. I qualify, being higher than hell on adrenaline and guilty of numerous serious errors in judgement.

But the Lord looks after pigs, too. And their judgement is just fine. A whiff of man scent on the eddying breeze, perhaps a foot slooping out of the mud, and there is a snort and a great rush in the sawgrass. A rush in the opposite direction.

I need a place to sit, but the nearest spot is a stump somewhere off in those trees, five thousand yards away. So I stand instead, swatting at the gnats that are beginning to explore the interiors of my ears and nose. The grass moves again, and sends blood rushing up into my head.

But it's just Gibbes—God bless him—on the tail end of a mile-long stalk. He works his way through the last forty yards of sawgrass, stalking to the very end. Even right at my side, he speaks in a whisper. "Got your wind at the last minute," he says, wiping a glob of mud from his temple. It leaves a long black streak down the side of his face. "Hog's got a nose like a bear," he says with a weary grin. "Peg you in a second." Gibbes looks over my shoulder, way out to middle distance. Far off somewhere, a gator bellows like an old outboard that won't quite start. A marsh hen cackles to the changing tide. "Let's get back to the boat," he says. "We'll grab us a bite, then float up a creek on the rising tide. There's a little spot I want to try."

It sounds good to me. Gibbes takes up the long trail where we left his skiff nosed up into the marsh. There we swap hog stories over lunch—Po' Boy sandwiches, sardines, crackers, and that sweet nectar of Carolina, strong and dark iced tea. The tide, now an hour into flood, courses through little creeks, murmuring and humming through the spartina. Oysters and barnacles pop and crackle in the rising water. In other places, pigs feed at dawn and dusk. Out here on the sea islands, they are more like marine animals, venturing from thickets to root and graze on low-water tidal flats, no matter the time of day.

Gibbes noses the wind and lays out a campaign. There is this sweeping bend in the river, he says, with a broad and flat expanse of what he calls "high marsh." High marsh does not describe prevalent vegetation, but rather the ground—such as it is—beneath. High marsh has a high content of sand—slightly on the solid side of Jell-O, like concrete making up its mind to set. A man can walk there, maybe keep his kneecaps out of the slop.

Gibbes cranks the outboard and hums us downriver a few miles, idles down, then eases his skiff onto the creekbank at a gator slide. It is another perfect spot for a man to consider his mortality—a spot worn bare by numerous saurians' downhill treks to food and safety. I put my feet where gator feet have very recently been, and struggle up the slippery bank.

We have seen a dozen gators on our trip downriver. They lie in the sunshine, impassive as logs, soaking up BTUs. Then—when we come too close for reptilian comfort—they ease into the safety of deep water. One was longer than our skiff. Eight, nine hundred pounds? His belly bulged from his last meal. He looked like a crocodile on an African travelogue.

There is something inscrutable about a gator. You can face down a bear, a wolf, a cougar. Look into those eyes and you'll likely know what lies behind them. Hunger? Fear? Indecision? Something will give you the answer. But a gator? A gator has the intelligence of a chicken, of a digital watch. And those yellow eyes will tell you nothing, nothing at all.

But I see only gator sign on that trek through the high marsh. Gibbes leads the way down a well-used game trail. Our tracks fall atop knife-edged deer tracks, atop the rounder, shorter cloven marks of pigs, atop coon prints like the tiny hands on my own birth certificate.

The spartina gradually gives way to needlegrass, and finally to broomsedge, as the land slowly creeps above the high water mark. We round a long scrubby point, studded with the bleached and gnarled remains of ancient trees. Beyond is a long salty swamp, and way out in the middle is a half-acre of open ground, churned black by rooting hogs. Gibbes stops in his tracks, reaches, finds my arm. I hold my ear inches from his lips. He whispers, "Cut a little to your left. Play the wind. Watch the eddy around that patch of pine." There is a final bit of advice: "Remember, you ain't sneaking up on deaf hogs."

Indeed, I am not. I ease through terrain where a panther would make a racket. The muck in the game trail sucks and slurps at my boots. If I strike out through the tall grass, I will make a noise like wading through a pile of Venetian blinds. I compromise, keeping to the trail but stepping on dry rooty clumps on either side. It's like walking along a ditch, one foot on either side.

But it works. Sort of.

There are pigs out there, but again, I cannot see them. Some sixth sense tells them of slurping danger. They ease off into the "can't see." I sneak to the edge of the clearing and hear snorting in the thicket to my left.

Then, there is movement. Black on black. A thirty-pound hog, too young to know all about pig-slaying Gibbes McDowell, picks his way across the mud. Right out there in the open. Another follows. I turn and look at Gibbes, now fifty yards behind me. "Short," I say with my hands. Then I hold up two fingers.

Return sign language tells me what I need to know. The little Mauser does its job. I do not hear the quick shots, but the other pigs do. They snort and grunt in surprise. Gibbes wears a hog call around his neck. He reaches for it, blows, but it issues only a muted hiss. A bit of sawgrass? An inconvenient glob of New River mud? Gibbes pulls the call apart, quickly fiddles with it. Another hiss, another lost opportunity. The hogs mill around for a long instant, then crash off into never-never. Into next time.

We sling the two downed pigs over our shoulders and slog toward the creekbank. There we will dress and wash them, keeping our eyes peeled for cruising gators. There I will dream of glowing piles of charcoal, of heavy sweet rolling hickory smoke, of Carolina yellow barbecue sauce, heavy with honey and mustard.

And of the tusks I did not get. Of the tusks I now know I will someday come back for. As surely as the moon pulls salt water up into the New River marsh, something will pull me back.

And I will come.

In the Valley of the Little Knife

The first bird blows out of the buffalo brush and hawthorn, a cackling rainbow of head, neck and wing, stretching and climbing the air, rising into the Dakota blue, then swinging downhill and downwind, as pheasants always do. I get on him with my old Sterlingworth, give him eighteen inches, then twenty-four. It's a heavy, long-barrelled twelve and you can't get a dime down either choke. But it's stocked straighter than most. Good for missing clays, deadly on birds.

Time runs like honey while I hold history in my hands. Roosevelt is president, there's a depression cooking and soup kitchens steaming and folks standing in line. Mr. Ansley H. Fox is broke and Savage buys him out, and up in Utica they are boxing the gun and shipping it south. Double triggers and no ejectors, off to Macon or Marietta or Mobile, to a hardware store smelling of rope, roofing tar, mule liniment and harness oil. Then somebody buys it for two weeks' wages even though he could have had a Browning or a Model 12 for less.

Surely he is a gentleman, in sentiment, at least. I do not know his name, but I know he's a big man since he adds a spacer and a recoil pad. He has large rough hands that wear the blueing thin and the checkering smooth, but he loves this gun and he oils the stock till the recoil pad petrifies. He shoots low base sevens and high base fours and sometimes buckshot, but he does not shoot her loose. Seventy-five years later, the pad bites my shoulder as I crumple a pheasant at thirty yards with an ounce-and-a-quarter of number fives.

North Dakota. You will know this country and love it even though it is not your own. Locals joke about "life in the *vast* lane," where the telephone pole is the state tree and the mosquito the state bird. Where they use a twenty-foot log chain for a weather vane, and where there are so many missile silos, a dose of Secession fever would make this place the world's third-largest nuclear power.

More truth than humor there. And if you did not laugh when you thought of megatons and Mutually Assured Destruction, you would lie down and weep the bitterest of tears. But that's another North Dakota, way up on the high ground, where half the landscape is sky, where the abandoned farmsteads and the one-room schools stand empty and forlorn and the prairie rolls beyond the curve of the world.

You are down where the Missouri and the Little Missouri and the Knife and the Little Knife slice through the hills, deep in a wonderment of creeks and springs and brushy coulees, where there are sometimes buffalo and wild horses and always coyotes and turkeys and ducks and deer and pheasants and sharptail grouse.

Lewis and Clark came a-westering here in 1804. "The country we passed is the same as yesterday," Meriwether Lewis noted in his journal, "beautiful in the extreme." They called this place Goat Pen Creek, from the fences the Indians made of aspen palings to corral driven antelope, whose skin is as soft as chamois. The Indians called it The River of the Little Knives.

The Little Knife wends its way from the Mountrail County

high ground, a little south of a farm town named Stanley, and dumps into the Missouri at Sanish Bay, "the home of a friendly people." The Indians walked the banks of the Missouri, following Lewis and Clark upstream. The last Indians were Teton Sioux and no white man wanted to rush right ashore. "Who are you?" they called from their canoes. The Indians shrugged. "*Arikara!*" they answered in their native tongue. "It is us!"

As I pick up that first bird, a ruffle of color in dun stubble, I see a field stone, one side blackened by an ancient campfire, and I know the Arikara—"the Ree," they call them in these parts—have been here as well. Then there are two quick shots and a whoop way down in the coulee where Miss Susan is dogging up the birds.

Miss Susan is tall and blonde and from East Tennessee and she grew up taking long steps on hilly ground. She's hunted birds in places I can't even pronounce. She took a kudu in Tanzania and a red stag in New Zealand and assorted other critters along the way. Then she took up with me and we took off to North Dakota, a place she could scarcely imagine, East Africa notwithstanding. "We're going after birds in South Dakota!" she'd crow to her friends.

"North," I'd say. "Think north!"

Indeed, talk about pheasants and most folks think south— South Dakota. Ditto for mulies and whitetail and sharptail and ducks, not to mention the geese and the exquisite fishing in the impoundments along the Big Muddy. But North Dakota has everything its southern neighbor does—except the numbers of hunters. Fly or drive another three hundred miles and you'll have the country all to yourself.

So Miss Susan thought north and we went north, by boat

and truck and plane and then another plane and finally by truck again, lugging guns and shells and boots and too many clothes since you never know how Dakota weather might do you, north to this valley of the Little Knife. Now she works north again, north along the riverbank with a Gordon setter named Molly, waist-deep in briars. The bushes thrash before her as the dog works hard to snuffle up a bird, and a long hank of tailfeathers trails from the back of her shooting vest. Beyond the river, way off where the land rises toward the ashy and aspened brow of the hills, a fine plume of dust hangs in the October air. It's ten-fifteen and Fred Evans is on his way out from the ranch house with coffee and cookies.

You can call Fred the Pheasant Nazi, a term he does not entirely appreciate. He'll wake you at six with a flare pistol shot over the top of your bunkhouse, sic Miss Joyce on you and she'll drown you with fresh-ground coffee from the Blue Mountains of Jamaica, feed you bacon and pancakes till you can hardly walk. Then Fred will drive you out in the bird bus and set you busting birds out of the bottomland in the morning, and up the ridge to run them back downhill come afternoon. It's burgers or barbecue lunchtimes, great platters of beef and the birds you shoot for supper, homemade cookies and the aforementioned coffee at 10:00 a.m. and 3:00 p.m. sharp. And after sundown when the dog men are dressing the birds, Fred will spin you up a couple of stories all dripping with history and wisdom, then check the dogs and the horses one last time and cast his eye along his pasture fences and still be stomping around the yard long after the coyotes have sung you to sleep. You can call Fred Evans the Pheasant Nazi if you want, but you'd better not, 'cause you're on the Triple T and the Triple T is his spread.

Triple T, says the sign on a fencepost corner. *Things Take Time*. Fred and Joyce's time here has been well spent. Four thousand acres and four hundred head, cows and calves and horses and hay and wheat and canola and machinery and sheds and the lazy Little Knife through the middle of it all, easing its way down to the Missouri, sighing like a river does when it's got something to say.

You'll know the story even if you cannot hear the words—this great tale of the prairie, the cow barons and railroad schemers and sod busters and all that came before. The buffalo trails you can still see along the knife-edged ridges, their wallows like darkening dimples when the sun slips down the sky and the light hits the ground sideways. Memories of the great and ancient nation of hunters that followed those herds, the painted men who rode bareback into battle and the four hundred years of teepee stones they left here and there in Fred's pasture, rings and rings upon the land.

Fred and Joyce are heirs to all of this. Fred walks like he grew up in the saddle. Joyce cooks like she is expecting a threshing crew, and you can read Finn in the fine lines of her face, hear it in her lilting brogue. "We are all put somewhere," Fred likes to say, and he firmly believes he and Joyce were put here for a good reason. The Triple T may be a working ranch, subject to the crushing numbers of modern agriculture, but about eight years ago, Fred Evans diversified.

Call it heeding a higher call. He farms for wildlife. He plants corn he will not harvest along the river and the little creeks that feed it. He rolls up big bales of wheatstraw with plenty of grain left in it and sets them out for feeders. He keeps an eye on the deer and the sharptails, rifles the coyotes whenever he can, turns loose pheasants that mix with their wild cousins and pretty soon take up their wily ways. And every year when he gets his crop up and gets the cows out on high-ground pasture till the snow drives them back downhill, Fred Evans lets a chosen few come out to educate his deer and birds.

We have done some serious educating this morning, and Fred sets up the chairs and lays out the cookies and passes out the cups and wants to know all about it. We pile the birds into the box bolted to the front bumper of the bus, sit and recite a litany of the ones we missed. The rooster that scared the beje-sus out of Miss Susan when he launched himself from between her knees. The roosters sparring in the stubble, so bent on eye-gouging and throat-slashing that they would not fly. Those birds in heavy cover we could not find, those birds in cover so heavy even the dogs could not find them, birds that blew up behind us after we had passed and stopped to mop a brow or catch a breath. The birds that buzzed the dogs where you dared not shoot or flew into the sun where you would not because you could not tell cock from hen.

Fred listens, commiserates. But when we shift gears to the shots we made, his commentary slides off toward the sarcastic. "These birds are kinda easy," he says with a devilish grin. Then he turns toward the distant hills and points with his nose the way an Indian might. "How about I take you up there after lunch and show you some sharptails?"

"All we got is number fives," I say. "They be good enough?"

"Don't matter what you shoot," Fred says, his grin now dangerously crowding his ears. "Your shot won't even catch up with 'em."

If we were educating pheasants along the Little Knife before lunch, after noon in the hills above, the sharpies send us back for post-graduate work. Fred leaves the road and works his way uphill, the bird bus creaking and rolling like a prairie schooner, tires losing traction on the grass, then finding it again. Higher and higher, past derelict horse-drawn hay rakes and plows, past the steel-wheeled tractor that pulled them when horses were just sweet nickering memories, up and up till the bird bus would go no more. "Sometimes you'll find singles," Fred says as he passes out the guns, "sometimes you'll find coveys in a patch of brush, sometimes around a pile of field stones, sometimes right out in the open."

"You're telling me they're unpredictable?" I ask.

"Sometimes they are," he says. "And they're just like crows. One is always watching."

A quarter-mile on foot, me in a swale knee-deep in the whispering tall grass, Miss Susan working the knob above, a cannonball of a bird whizzes by my head. I swing right to left, a shot I seldom make.

"What was that?" Miss Susan hollers from the heights.

"Damned if I know," I reply.

It is the one Fred was talking about, the one always watching. Five steps later, three dozen birds take wing before Susan's gun. Two shots and one falls and the rest of the covey climbs the wind, then swings down to ride it, high over my head. I lead the first bird a good four feet and the second bird falls.

"Good shot," Susan hollers. "How far did you lead him?"

"Fourteen feet!" I holler back.

After supper we gather on the porch, scratched up, wore down, and satisfied. The birds cackle goodnight in the hedges at the edge of the ranch yard and the coyotes strike up a great and mournful chorus somewhere out in the hills.

"North Dakota," Miss Susan says, looking out at the valley of the Little Knife, the shadows growing long upon the land. "I had no idea."

"How many people are out here, Fred?" I ask.

He pauses, looks out to where the hills become sky. The coyotes drift off to about nothing and the hoot owls take up asking questions. "About six hundred thousand, and half of them live in just four towns. The rest of us are spread pretty thin."

"How far is it to town?"

He grins. "Fifty-six miles to the Wal-Mart door."

"And your kids?" Susan asks.

"One day they walked up that bluff and saw there was a big old world out there...."

"Somebody said North Dakota's children are your most valuable export," I say.

"I heard that once," he says, the sadness almost hidden in the spaces between words. He turns and waves his hand along the horizon, glorious now with the sun slipping away and the clouds making great lavender canyons of air. "But some things are more important than this."

The coyotes take it up again and you know Fred Evans may be right about a lot of things, but he is dead wrong about this.

And the sky fades from purple to violet to beyond human sight and the Big Dipper wheels and you find the North Star and it is right above you and you know if the weather holds, you will have another day like this tomorrow.

Born Meat in a Dry Season

It's so dry you can't remember what rain smells like and the squirrels make a racket till you think Stonewall Jackson's army is foraging in the woods.

My third night on the stand. Two does the first night, nothing the second. But the wind has swapped directions and it feels like rain and if you listen close, you can hear the surf way off in the distance, way out on the front beach, working hard to mumble up a storm.

Leaves crackle and I thumb the safety and slowly turn toward the noise. I see only the scrub palmettoes stretching off toward the slash pine at the edge of the swamp, the glorious live oak canopy, and the Spanish moss hanging like long gray strings of tears.

Daufuskie's deer season is the nation's longest, from the fifteenth of August to the first of the year—no deer tag and no limit on bucks and you can hunt an hour before sunrise to an hour after sunset and kill two does a day most weekends.

You can figure on getting your venison in October when cooler weather beats back the bugs and slows up the gators and drives the snakes underground. But the sea trout and redfish might be running and the marsh hens cackling for the gun, and right across the Georgia line upwards of a million quail are whistling and you might get distracted and pretty soon you'll be out of red meat.

That's where I was when I broke out the stand and hung it in a soft maple way back where the live oaks drop their mast and steal the sky and thin the cassena and wax myrtle so you can see to shoot if a buck slips out of the swamp for acorns in the late afternoon.

But damn, it was still so dry and the weather too warm and the gnats would eat you alive if you sat long in the woods. I had this string of cedar decoys and some old double guns and duck season was coming up and I heard there were a couple of ponds over on Turtle Island. So I got to thinking how it might be in nasty weather with the ducks driven off the big water, shooting widgeons and scaup and pintails and if I was real lucky, maybe a couple of mallards.

"Where you all gone?" Ronnie asked. He spoke Gullah, the gentle patois of slaveship, blues, and voodoo. Our seventeen-foot Whaler was idling and the tide was an hour into the ebb, the seabound water sucking and swirling and gurgling around the base of the pilings.

There was me and Robert Senior and Robert Junior and Ronnie. Both Roberts were visiting for a spell and had a hankering for some ducking later on, if it would ever rain and turn cold and the birds would make it this far south.

Ronnie is fifth-generation. He knows where to pick clams and oysters and conch and where to get mullet and shrimp with a cast net. He can tell you about storms and tides and the phases of the moon and he ain't at all stingy with it. "Turtle Island," I said.

"Turtle Island? Ain't nothing there but sand and coon and snake."

"We looking for ducks," I said. "You know those ponds behind the beach?"

We were on the county dock. Across salt marsh the color of ripening wheat, through the haze kicked up by the breakers, you could just make out a ship in the Savannah channel, red and white and inbound.

The Gullah call it *compersation*. Ask them something they don't want to answer and they'll ask the question right back to you. Ask them the wrong question and they'll give you the answer to the question you should have asked—*axed*—in the first place. "How you gone get there?"

"Poke around on the high tide and find a way to come ashore."

Ronnie sucked his teeth and shook his head. "Tide drappin' now. You watch out, or it leave you till mornin'."

"Where those ponds?"

"Bout shree-quarter mile puntop Savannah River." *Puntop* means above, or close to, or maybe on the other side of.

"How about the beach?"

Ronnie grunted and looked out to the southeast. "It get mean if the wind come up. Why you gone there?" He knew the answer, but this was compersation, so he could axe again.

"Ducks," I said again.

"Ducks? It's mos' December, man, you best get yo-sef some born meat."

"What you mean, Ronnie?"

"Born meat. You know, possum or coon or deer."

"When weather bus' loose," I said, trying out my Gullah.

"Well, don' let em bus' loose on Turtle Island. An' watch out for them rattlehead coppermouth. They mos' big as boar constructor."

The river wound southeast across the flats, turning sometimes almost back upon itself. The spartina moved in the seawind, reeds bearing marks of the falling water. The tide caught the keel and the engine fluttered and the boat skittered like a car on a rainslick road.

Then there was one more bend, and then the sea, the gray and greasy heaving swells, the surf torn and plunging on the outer bars, the mist over all of it and the green smudge of islands stretching down towards St. Augustine and beyond.

Turtle Island was a dozen low hummocks, two acres, five, ten, strung like turquoise beads along a bright foamy beach. We read the surf from the ocean side, a hard thing to do.

Robert Senior was at the helm. "How much water we got?"

I squinted at the depth finder. "Six feet." We were still a quarter-mile offshore.

The swells were starting to curl, the way they do when the bottom comes up slow. I eyed a spot where the breakers didn't seem too bad. "Bear for that driftwood snag," I said. Two hundred yards to go, the prop started kicking sand.

Robert Senior brought her around right before the breaker caught us. I slipped over the side, waist-deep in the froth, fighting to keep the bow into the waves and my feet out of the prop.

Robert Senior gave the helm to his son and joined me overboard. We slogged ashore, while Robert Junior did a passable job of getting the Whaler off the beach.

Snake pistol in hand, and Robert Senior in tow, we looked *puntop*. The relentless ocean had broached the first pond, and it was no longer any more than a surging bay. The second pond was a half-acre brackish disappointment, but then we saw the patch of water trees—soft maple, gum and tupelo, all yellow and red with the season, way up in the pines.

We walked up the dunes, through the rustling palmetto thickets, eyes peeled for rattlehead coppermouths, up into the pines to the hardwoods beyond. Half a mile and we struck a trail of coon tracks like the hands of tiny children. And then Robert Senior whistled softly. "Look at this."

All at once, I forgot about ducks. The tracks of a deer were pegged to the dewclaws in the soft sand, tracks fully as big as a pack of smokes. Now, we have boodles of deer on these islands, but entangled genetics and a steady diet of salt scrub make a 150-pound buck a rarity. There are exceptions, monstrous animals, slipping through the saltmarsh to bed on brushy cedar hummocks well before *day-clean*, bucks seldom seen and never, ever brought to the gun. "He's a big old boy," Robert said, tracing the lines with his finger. "His hooves got the sharp worn right off them."

The tracks skirted the edge of the backwash and the tide was *drappin'*, so we knew the trail was only ten minutes old. It led to an acre of mud, with two deep wallows that somehow still held water. A thin line of bubbles blubbered from a hollow beneath a stump. Robert eyed my pistol. "What you got in that thing?"

"Snakeshot," I said.

"Well, if a bull gator comes boiling out at us, you shoot for his eyes. I'll write you a damn fine eulogy."

But I wasn't thinking about dying, not just yet. There was a fine tall magnolia downwind and I thought of coming back with rifle and stand, of slogging ashore and sitting here until the buck came to drink the only fresh water on Turtle Island.

So we worked our way back to the beach and hailed Robert Junior ashore.

Back outside the breakers, soaked again to our armpits, we laid a campaign. I would pack lunch and maybe supper, gather rope and knives and snakebite kit and bug dope. They would bring me back on the next day's tide, and pick me up after it was too dark to shoot.

But the morning brought a freshening wind and memories of Ronnie's *compersation* and I considered the dead-cinch scenario—the sun setting and the light failing and the wind and surf rising and me stuck on the island with scant vittles and no whiskey and a ripening buck with those gators and rattlehead coppermouths and the plague of salt marsh mosquitoes descending on me in great biting hordes.

So I called Robert Senior and told him he and his boy could have that Turtle Island buck all to themselves. They took one look at the breakers and begged off, too.

So now I'm slipping off into the woods, not two hundred yards behind my shack on the banks of the Cooper River, when a pickup comes rattling down the road. Leroy is at the wheel. I see him and he sees me and he locks up his brakes, cuts a quick U-turn and gives me the evil eye through the considerable dust he raises.

There is a tradition on Daufuskie, the sacred ritual of the Saturday night beach fire for the Last Gasp crowd down at Mudbank Mammy's, where the gumbo's hot and the beer's cold and the juke box free and they sweep up the eyeballs at closing time. Locals stand and spit and stare morosely into the flames and by and by somebody invariably throws on an armload of treated lumber. You can look in his eyes and figure this: Leroy has spent too much time downwind.

Ronnie calls him *Cider*. Homicider? Suicider? "Ain't no tellin', but they'll be a plantin' somebody befo' too long."

Leroy had a girlfriend once, but she turned him loose after they got into a domestic discussion and he livened up her vodka with Drano. She slopped some onto the counter and figured not to drink it when she saw the linoleum blister and crawl. Leroy pulled a gun on a neighbor who took offense at the barkeeping, then dumped five gallons of drain oil on the post office steps after the sheriff sent him papers in the mail. So I thank the bushes swishing shut behind me and wonder what the hell's got him riled up this time.

And then I remember. The well-marked trail that leads through the scrub magnolia down to the palmettoes and big oaks where I have my stand, the rumpled dry leaves, the broken branch, the bit of flagging tape tied to the cassena. I figured it was from another hunter and now I figure it was Leroy.

So I sit an hour in these glorious woods and then there is a great crackling rush and a doe streaks through the woods, a great blur of ears and hooves and hair, right at the bottom of the stand. Two heartbeats and there is another rush and I see the sun flash yellow off the antlers. There is no time for the scope and I swing like I might have swung on a Turtle Island pintail and shoot at ten feet.

There on my knees in the dry leaves, elbow-deep in my field-dressing chores, I think of a debt I owe. I am not on Turtle Island, stranded by rising surf and rising wind. I have not been snakebit, gator-gnawed. I am not dragging a buck that will surely sour before I ever get to eat it. So Ronnie will get a hind quarter of this deer, this born meat.

I slice and whittle and pull as the shadows lengthen and the light fades. Way off in the woods, the turkeys cluck and mew and gobble, gathering to roost in the tall pines.

I will drag this buck to the road and labor him into my truck and I will drive down to Mudbank Mammy's and beg five gallons of ice to fill his body cavity and I will tarp him up and skin and butcher him in the morning. I do not know it yet, but there at the beer joint back door I will see Leroy's former girlfriend, the one with no stomach for Drano. And I will tell her where I shot it and she will laugh and say, that's where Leroy has his marijuana patch. And then I'll know that Leroy made that trail hauling water in this driest of seasons, that he walked in from the east to keep me off his plants and the deer winded him and took off west and I got my piece of born meat. But I do not know this as I drag the buck out to the road while raindrops the size of dimes begin spattering into the thirsty ground. It is so dry, the first of them raise dust.

A Child in the Way She Shall Go

Miss Laura wades into the foaming backwash, stops just before the water gets to her cut-off jeans, winds up and flings her bottom rig far out into the breakers. There's seven feet of graphite and two hundred yards of twenty-pound line on a Penn 309 with a four-once sinker and two three-ought hooks and cut finger mullet on the business end.

The line cuts a perfect arc over the rubble of rolling water. The sinker comes down, but the line stays tight and I know she is thumbing the spool like I taught her, reading distance and wind and weight and the strength of her own long-armed throw, playing the Penn like a Cajun fiddle. Five seconds, ten, and the bait is on the bottom. She flips the lever, takes up the scant slack, then holds the rod in the crook of her arm while she works cigarettes from a pocket way too tight for them. She grabs her lighter, cups it against the wind and there is a flash of yellow as a cloud of smoke sails down the breeze.

Way out across the inlet, through the wind-driven scud, Tybee Island lies like a fine green smudge along the edge of the world. Blurs of beach houses peek through the treeline and above it all there's the Tybee Light, black and white and faithful, sentinel of the Savannah ship channel. The gulls wheel and the ocean crawls and the surf thunders while the tide sings, and way out to the east a freighter swings around a sea buoy and heads for port while the sun slides down the copper sky.

I watch Laura fish and realize I have finally found the perfect woman, a woman who packs a pistol and drives a four-by-four and who can string a fence and break a horse and butcher fish and kill a buck and drag him home and hang and skin him and fry me chops the next morning. She's bright and witty and tiny and beautiful and I love her with a ferocity I hardly knew an old man still had.

Miss Laura Elaine Lyseng Pinckney, the littlest girl with the longest name, is my daughter. The Good Book almost got it right. "Raise up a child in the way that he shall go, and he will not depart from it." My own momma considers my life—the years and the miles and the women and the whiskey and the land and time frittered away—and pronounces that verse the vilest of heresies. But if you drop *he* and plug in *she*, you'll come up with the Gospel Truth.

There is a whole bunch to tell you now, and I don't know quite where to begin. About growing up here in South Carolina and heading out for Alaska and breaking down in Minnesota and buying that run-down farm when I realized I did not have to go all the way to The Great Land in order to see wolves and moose and to freeze to death. About cutting wood and rolling rocks and raising cows and horses and of the woman who ran off with the hired man and left me flat-footed and heartbroke about the time the first snow came. About that long lonesome winter and the spring thaw when I first dared date again. And about meeting Laura's momma up in Fargo, North Dakota, and having her out to ride a spirited mare and how the mare blew up and the woman lay in the ditch with a shattered femur and said "Roger, I think this is going to cramp our sex life."

And how I rode home and put up the horses and came back with a rope and a board and how she screamed when I straightened her leg and lashed it down and how I dragged her to the back of the pickup and drove her to the hospital. And the clawing guilt that bade me bring her back and set her on my porch and feed her while she mended.

But that broken leg proved no obstacle, and we named our daughter for Laura Ingalls, the little girl in the little house in the big woods. And now she stands, grown up and glorious, thigh-deep in rolling water, looking out on Tybee Roads, waiting on that first strike.

There are sharks in this surf—makos, tigers, and hammerheads—and sometimes you can see their shadows, long and dark like pine logs, hanging in the cusps of breakers. There are whiting and tarpon and redfish and stingrays—*stingerees*, we call them down here—devil-faced and as big as your kitchen table, and if you step on one and he nails you, you'll wish you'd got snakebit instead. Bait up with cut mullet and sling your rig out into this water on the evening floodtide and you will always catch something, but you can never be sure of just what.

The wind gathers sand and sends it hissing along the beach. It sounds like dry snow sliding off the tin roof of the barn I no longer own, and suddenly Minnesota's frozen fields and crystalline lakes and brooding spruce seem another world, someone else's life, but I know it was real when I look out and see Laura fishing the backwash.

The years in between were far harder than this telling. Laura's momma and I shared roof and bed and board, but little else. We grew older and grew apart and I would come in from evening chores when the aurora was crackling and rolling overhead and say, "Come on, honey, you've got to see this." And when she would not go, I would scoop Laura from her crib and bundle her against the deadly cold and walk far out into the yard and she would look up and coo with wonder and hide her face in the warmth of my neck and say, "I love you, Pa," just like Laura Ingalls would have said. Later, I taught her to hunt and taught her to fish and gave her a four-teen-foot skiff and a weedless three-horse we called The Salad Shooter and I set her loose upon fresh water the way my own father turned me loose upon salt. And I'd stay home and cook the grits and sharpen the knives while Laura got us supper. Or sometimes we'd fish together, father and daughter, for bream and crappies and big toothy pike, in sunny bays summertimes when the living was easy, through the ice in winter when it was not.

And her momma? Lordy, I loved her, but it just didn't seem to do me any good at all. I'll spare you the details, but I can tell you I was less of a man than I should have been. Through that long winter of our discontent—ten winters in calendar time—we talked and fought and wept, and when there was nothing left to do but leave, I sold the farm and set Laura and her momma up in a log house down by the lake.

The first six months were as painless as such a thing might be, but then I took up with another woman and Laura would lie in bed at night and cry because she thought I didn't love her any more. The judge ordered counseling and Laura and I sat in a sterile office and looked into the sterile eyes of the counselor and told her how much we loved each other. But she did not tell me and I did not tell her and when it all got too much for me, I sold and gave away almost everything I owned and packed my rods and tackle and guns and decoys and headed back to the Carolina lowcountry, coming full circle after thirty years. I settled in on Daufuskie, and took up this precarious business of writing for a living. And just when I thought I had lost her for good, Miss Laura called looking for a plane ticket and my soul leapt up within me. And I knew for the very first time that all my love was not in vain.

Now I watch the rod come alive and Laura throw down that cigarette and lean into the fish and I can hear her holler over the rumbling surf and I shout back, "Hold him, darlin', hold him!" And she does.

Once, twice, three times, the line cuts back and forth through the curling waves and I think "hog redfish, big drum." Laura labors over the Penn for ten minutes, then begins walking backwards, horsing the fish into shallow water. Then I see the fin and I know it's a sand shark.

She grabs it by the tail and flips it onto the beach before it can grab back. I fetch the tape and call it legal and Laura lays it on a driftwood stump and starts skinning it, working from the inside out to keep the edge on her blade. The surf thunders and the tide sings and way out in Tybee Roads, another ship heads for port.

Daybreak Monday Morning

A board the *Haig Point Osprey*. It's daybreak Monday and we are all a little hung over, but this is when the boat leaves and you got to be on time so we are.

There is me and J. T. and Lester and Jimmie. There's Newyork, too, but he's hit the weekend harder than the rest of us and now sleeps on a coil of rope, so you can't count him.

The *Osprey* is a Breaux Brothers forty-footer with twin Jimmies, fast, trim, and seaworthy, built in Louisiana to haul roughnecks out to the oil rigs. But that boom went bust and now she works here as another boom—houses and golf and real estate—careens into the abyss.

The mate casts off and the skipper slips the boat into gear, port engine forward, starboard in reverse, and the diesels rattle and the gears grumble and the hull hums like a bass fiddle far out of tune as we pivot around on our stern. Both engines forward now, we idle across the boat basin and break out into the channel and throttle up and head down the Savannah River toward the sea.

We're bound for Daufuskie, up the river, back in time. No bank, no doctor, no traffic on the other side, and no bridge to get you there. But there is the First African Baptist where spirituals still ring, there are shanties trimmed in blue to keep back the spirits, and cows tethered beneath spreading dooryard pecans. There are deer and alligators and turkeys and fields grown over with honeysuckle and briar and, around it all, the woods—magnolias loaded with blossoms big as hubcaps, vast temples of oak all weeping Spanish moss, and always the pines, weaving sad secrets of seabreeze. There's the lazy *swoosh* of lowtide surf, the thunder at high water, the seawind moving the saltmarsh like wheat, and a pewter path upon the waters when the moon creeps over the edge of the world.

This is home to the Gullah, heirs to slavery. This is home to sundry white people, artists and outlaws, painters and poets and shrimpers and retired dope smugglers, blown ashore for various reasons. But Hilton Head is right across the river and Daufuskie is also home to the would-be real estate potentates, the speculators, the developers who have left their marks along the ocean side—inns and horse stables and tennis courts and golf courses and million-dollar homes—plantations, they call them—where you can't go unless you belong.

There are beach clubs and cabanas, swimming pools and spas, ferries and buses and ten-dollar burgers and four-dollar beers, all adrift in red ink and indecision, victims to a jittery market and soft real estate, but especially to marine transportation, to boats like this, to winds and tides and things that break, to skippers who can't find deep water and to mudbanks where they are not supposed to be.

There were fortunes spent, fortunes lost, twenty years of bankruptcy, litigation and great corporate wreckage. But like a man who continues leaping from his roof, thinking he can fly if he just flaps a little harder next time, developers keep coming back. Today we haul screw guns, nail guns, trowels, hammers and miter saws. We haul ladders and wrenches and bolts, screws and nails and men.

I am on my way home from Savannah pleasures—library, pub and pizza, things we do not have on Daufuskie. These men are on their way to work, building what we do not have there either—a highrise condominium, our first. My neighbors put me up to going to court to stop it. I did what I could and I lost. Seven months and seven million lost, J. T. and Jimmie and Lester do not begrudge me my conscience. And I do not begrudge them their wallets. We are just four men on the stern of the *Haig Point Osprey*, two black, two white, nursing cigarettes and coffee, chewing over the scenery we pass.

A storm rolled through around midnight, rumbling in from the sea, booming over the islands like truckloads of empty barrels, and now a mist lies heavy on General Oglethorpe's dream. Savannah—geometric, green and wonderful. The tinkling fountains, the sleepy tree-lined boulevards, the green commons and the great river itself exhale a collective and aromatic essence of history and grief that rises past roof and spire and hangs in the stillness of the morning like some fine blue aura. The sad old buildings along River Street where cotton and slaves were sold, the rainslick wrought iron and brick and ballast stone, catch the rising sun and glow like the Lord's burning rage.

We pass what is left of the *Barba Negra*, a jumble of masts and spars and booms rising from the dark singing water. She's one of the last of the old square-riggers, once a North Sea coastal freighter, then a Savannah tourist attraction before some gal's panties wound up in the bilge pump. Her skipper was off somewhere and by the time he got back, *Barba Negra* was on the bottom and a couple of gators had taken residency in her hull.

I could tell you now about her skipper, how he once got too close to Russia and got thrown in a Siberian jail. How he's been in hurricanes and typhoons and maybe mutinies and how he fell out of the rigging one night and broke his ankle and hobbled aft and stood on one leg and stayed at the helm. But then I would have to tell you about this city's long love for deep blue water, about Captain Flint laid up and dying on Broad Street, crying out for rum with his last breath, about the Waving Girl, the lonely sister of a lighthouse keeper, seduced by a sailor who swore he'd come back, who met every incoming ship—flag by day and lantern by night—for the next forty years.

I could tell you about the runaway slaves on the islands we pass, about the men who went out to capture them and never came back, and of the last load of wild Africans, smuggled up this river in 1858, put to cotton with bare hoe-handles since they were judged yet too fierce for steel. I could tell you of the messianic fervor that swept through the freedmen after the Quake of '86, how men quit their fields and women sewed ascension robes and many Jesuses arose from among them, how most were incarcerated but one escaped to New York City and became Father Divine, gathering three million followers until he ran afoul of the IRS. I could tell you all of this, but I would be forever on the stern of this crewboat, forever watching my cigarette smoke slide down the river breeze, and never get to the rest of the story, poised now for me to give it life and breath.

So I will just tell you about the gators, how they had that skipper boogered, how the grand old *Barba Negra* just lay there on her side, slowly coming loose at the seams, a roost for herons, a fish drop, a wildlife refuge, the mermaid carved upon her bow bearing a broad swipe of oily scum across her lovely wooden nipples.

"How come he don't get her up?" Jimmy asked. "Them cannons could shoot a beer can clean across the river." The front of his hardhat read, "WWBD?" and the fine print beneath it, "What Would Bubba Do?"

I told him about the gators.

Jimmie is from red clay country where there are no gators. He gets up at four and makes the crewboat a little after six. "Ain't no gators in downtown Savannah," he proclaims, half believing, eyeing the dark beneath the timbers beneath the dock across the quay.

Lester is tall and dark and blacksnake skinny. "No gators?" he spits over the side, "Boy, let me tell you something. Remember them men who used to live 'neath the Talmadge Bridge? They come up short two or three one mornin' an' po-leece say bull gator snatch 'em clean out they card-bode box."

We pass grassy berms, a pentagon of brick, cannons here and there along the parapets, fortifications which kept the British and later the Yankees away from Savannah. The British gave up but the Yankees came back a century later, with money instead of guns, and now own what General Sherman could not keep. And now when you're stuck in traffic and read the plates you'll wonder how in all creation there is anybody left in Ohio. And then the skipper throttles back as we overtake the *Dresden Empress*, outbound.

She's huge and square and ugly, three city blocks long, a dozen decks above water, who knows how many below, all up in gantries and container freight like truck vans. There is no bare-breasted mermaid upon her bow, but there is mystery about her anyway—the hum of her engines, the roil of smoke from her stack, the obscure flags slapping from her stern. We speak of ships like these—Singapore-built of Korean steel, European-owned, Liberian-registered, with Greek officers, Hindu engineers, and the babble of many nations when the crew hits the River Street dives. And then a woman, as they generally do, turns the mystery into magic.

She leaves the bridge and walks forward along the port rail. She is as brown as Lester, maybe as tall. We cannot see the color of her dress there in the river glare, but it's dark and we imagine it purple as it falls to her ankles and plays in the wind, and we ache as we watch her move. And there is a flash of fire when her face catches the sun and I figure it's a necklace, hand-hammered of Congo gold, but J. T. says it's a tooth and he has better eyes than me.

J. T. and I wound up together on this boat this morning by accident. He had left me a note on the other side, down at Freeport, the beer and burger joint on the Cooper River, where this crew eases the hour between quitting time and boat time. But that evening J. T. was already on the boat and Mr. Edgar was presiding at the bar, speaking of a man we have come to call Naked Jim. "He likes to get drunk," Edgar paused for effect, "and get naked. He was drunk and buck-naked over in Bluffton and the po-leece came and he said 'damnit, can't a man get drunk and buck-naked in his own front yard?' And when they told him he couldn't, he went out and bought an island down in the Keys so he could get drunk and naked there."

Mr. Edgar was himself drunk but not naked, and clearly enjoying his own tale. He's about half-size, pushing fifty, with a small, kind face and quick eyes that warn you when he's about to get tangential. And they were dancing that evening. "Here," he said, "somebody left something for you."

He passed me a scrap torn from a bar tab. There was a Savannah phone number, the initials J. T., and a cryptic note. "I hear you write a book," it said. "Call about my uncle."

"Hope you don't mind," Edgar said. "He said it was some kind of family history."

I did mind. At least at first. I had written four books but I was nursing each of them along, buying beer and beans off magazine articles, and had about all I could do to sell my own stuff. But then I got to thinking about maybe some great literary work was just lying there undiscovered so I called the number and J. T. and I played phone tag for a week.

We finally connected, and by and by I got a package from Sheridan, Wyoming, a curious and massive manuscript about a man pursued by spirits wanting to induct him into the Flying Africans. Now, we have a few flying Africans down here, when the beer is cold and the jukebox is hot, but they generally don't fly as high as they used to, when legend says they took wing from plantations from the Edisto to the Altamaha and maybe Daufuskie, too, flying back to Africa and to freedom.

J. T.'s uncle apparently has a way of showing up unexpectedly, defying the laws of hitchhiking and Greyhound. "He was staying at my brother's up in Georgetown," J. T. says, "and he called asking for a ride to the bus station. My brother knocked off and drove home and couldn't find him anywhere. He was hollering around the house for him when the phone rang. My uncle was already in Savannah."

We are swinging into Wall's Cut, a boneyard of driftwood,

where the logs and snags and even whole trees washed all the way from the great Blue Ridge Mountains lie in a jumble along the shore, roots and branches raised in silent supplication, pleading for time to turn like the tide and give them sap and leaves and life once again.

"Damn," I say. "How long did it take?"

"Oh, about an hour or so."

Jimmie scratches his head and lights another smoke. "Two hundred miles an hour?" he asks.

I ask about the postmark on the manuscript. "How in the world did he wind up in Wyoming?"

J. T. looks off into middle distance. A porpoise broaches alongside the boat, blowing and eyeing us and smiling that little porpoise smile. "Same way he got to Savannah, I reckon." Then he leans forward so only I can hear. "Let me axe you something. You believe in this stuff?"

"J. T.," I say, "I grew up here same as you."

He knocks the ash off his cigarette, and, like Lester, says, "Let me tell you something." He pauses like Edgar did when he spoke of Naked Jim. "I was with a gal and I got tired of her company."

"Yeah?" I say.

"Yeah. So I took off walking. I walked behind houses, I walked through the woods, I walked places you couldn't drive a car. I walked clean across Savannah. I wound up at this other gal's place and spent the night, and daylight next mornin', there was the first gal knocking at the do'. She hauled me home and when I got there I seen my picture on the floor and seven candles lit and seven shiny dimes and some fool powder sprinkled all around."

"Huh," I say.

"And that ain't all," he says. "She poured all my licker in a big circle on the carpet. Why she do that?"

Lester had caught the last half of our conversation. "Was you drunk when you lef'?" he asks.

"Well, shore I was."

"Well, there you go," Lester says.

"Poured out all that good licker!" J. T. says, still mourning the loss.

Daufuskie is around the bend. It rises above oceans of spartina, the pines all wreathed in seamist, the oaks laying their branches over the edge of the salt marsh like young girls casting their hair to dry in the sun.

"Wake up, Newyork," Jimmie says.

Newyork rises to one elbow, shakes his head, and blinks at the morning, hard and bright as the light off a tin roof at high noon. The rope has left a braided pattern along one cheek. "I ain't been sleeping," he says, "I been talkin' to Jesus."

And the diesel rattles and dies and the dock creaks and our wake swooshes along the bank and the mark on his cheek looks like some ornate tribal scar.

Hiroshima on Main

The Old Man wobbled off Delta 760 at Minneapolis–St. Paul, punch drunk from altitude and Jack Daniels. He was eighty and a little shaky, even sober, even on solid ground.

There was the usual first class rush, then a long gap in the line while the crowd at the gate stirred and twitched and fretted. Then came the Old Man, survivor of his first commercial flight, survivor of the Great Depression and the Second World War. He had put himself through Carolina, lettering billboards saying *See Rock City*, *Chew Brown's Mule*, *Drink Dixie Cola*. But then there was Pearl Harbor and Saipan and Tinian and Luzon, and finally Okinawa.

My own history was scarcely less dramatic. I grew up across the river from Parris Island, and came to honky-tonk age with Marine Vietnam returnees. A drunken corporal told of thrusting the muzzle of his M-16 between the legs of a young Vietnamese girl, lifting her screaming and wriggling, threatening to pull the trigger unless her mother gave him oral sex. Another, of taking three villagers up in a chopper, and throwing two off before interrogating the third. A friend, crabbing for summer money, discovered the sodden remains of one of the proud, the brave, the few, who had toppled into the river after severing femoral arteries on razor wire strung to prevent his escape.

This is damned inconvenient to remember now, Marines being heroes in Afghanistan and Iraq. But this was 1965 and I swore I would not go.

When the dust finally settled, I remained a free man, but a virtual exile, finding refuge, finally, on a northern Minnesota farm.

My father's reaction was predictable and it was twenty years before I saw him again. And that's why we were in the airport that August afternoon.

We had another two hundred miles to go, but first, I offered the Old Man a whirlwind tour of the Twin Cities. We drove Summit and Grand Avenues, where he reckoned the homes of the robber barons were less impressive than those of southern slaveholders. We stopped at the monument to the Union dead across from St. Paul's Cathedral, where he refused to get out of the truck when I told him Minnesota volunteers had broken the great Confederate charge at Gettysburg. Noon found us on the banks of the Mississippi, walking brick streets in the oaken shade while the river murmured at our feet and the city rumbled above us. I was hungry and suggested lunch at a nearby Japanese restaurant.

"Is that," he asked, "one of those places where they chop the food at your table?"

I nodded.

There was a pause and then, "I'm sorry son, I can't get that close to a Jap with a knife."

And then he said, "It was on Saipan in forty-four. The Japanese headed north, took two thousand women and children with them. We dropped leaflets. We would open the lines and let civilians out. All they had to do was wear white."

He had orders to monitor the exodus. "I could see rivers of white," he said, "moving down the valley below me."

But the movement in the blasted jungle was not non-combatant. Soon, nearly every Japanese soldier on Saipan would come howling down upon unsuspecting Marines, in one great banzai charge into Eternal Glory.

"I seen them haul our men out of ambulances, the officers rip them open with their swords." He pointed a quarter-mile to the far bank. "I was as close as that."

"'What happened to the civilians?" I asked.

"They marched them off cliffs into the sea. Our ships tried to pick up the survivors, but their propellers fouled on the bodies."

We ate burgers and the Old Man fell asleep in the truck, twitching and mumbling through an old soldier's dreams.

It would be years before I discovered the rest of the story.

With the Marines that bloody June day was Robert Sherrod, a combat correspondent for *Time* and *Life*. After the rush of bayonets and long knives, Sherrod went to Marpi Point to investigate rumors of civilian deaths upon the cliffs. Sherrod, who had covered the war from Attu to Tarawa, was unprepared for what he saw. Hundreds of bodies—men, women, children—bobbing in the surf. And a few stragglers, ritually bathing before drowning, or wrapping themselves in flags before blowing themselves apart with hand grenades.

Sherrod staggered back to his typewriter. "Do the suicides of Saipan," he asked, " mean that the whole Japanese race will chose death before surrender?"

"The Nature of the Enemy" ran in *Time* in August, 1944. Translated and manipulated, it became a major Japanese propaganda exhortation, urging death rather than surrender.

Some Japanese embraced national self-destruction. The great hordes of kamikaze pilots that were to soon hurl themselves against American ships certainly believed.

And so did Harry Truman. Believing he was saving half a million American lives, he ordered the nuclear annihilation of Hiroshima and Nagasaki.

Our years echo with litanies of *what ifs* and *why nots*. Allow me others. What if the Old Man had been able to identify those multitudes and called down massive artillery fire? Would the attack have butchered the Marines? Would Robert Sherrod have written that piece that galvanized Japanese propagandists? What about Hiroshima? Nagasaki? The forty-year nuclear standoff with the Soviet Union? What about those missiles, surviving the recent flurry of goodwill between nations, that are still armed and ready, as we eat, sleep, make love and die?

Some things seem certain. History's turntable swings on an exceedingly fine axle. And all of us—Russian, American, Vietnamese, Japanese, Rebel and Yankee—are connected by the intricate web of life we have been given, and equally by the hateful entanglements we have created.

But now we have Kim Jung Il and maybe still Osama and at least one of them has a nuclear bomb. Macbeth said it best: "This even-handed justice commends the ingredience of our poisoned chalice to our own lips."

Those were some things I learned one horrible and lovely August afternoon a long time ago, while a great city went about its noontime business and the Father of Waters steadily sought the sea.

A Rage in the Tall Marsh Grass

"Hey Bro'," Silas said, "You see any-ting with white tail?"

"Possum?" I asked.

"How you talk, Bro'! I talkin' 'bout deer!"

We were hooked over the bar at Mudbank Mammy's, down on Daufuskie Island. Me and Silas and Billy. Tyler was tending bar and Beth was in the kitchen, slapping burgers and ladling gumbo. It was deep down in October, and way out across the high marsh the lights of Savannah almost stole the glory from the stars.

Silas is Gullah, a descendent of slaves, but now he is freer than any man I know. He knows where to get clams and oysters, when the shrimp and hog mullet run, and he's real handy with a cast net.

A little swatch of breeze came a-ghosting up the river and set the acorns rattling onto the roof. They rumbled down the tin and plooped into the palmetto scrub beneath the eaves. "Incoming," Billy said.

Billy has big hands and a big face and he looks at you with one eye while the other kind of wanders around and looks at things over your shoulder—a habit from 'Nam, he says, when he had to keep both eyes busy. Billy does pretty good, so long as he takes his pills and lays off the whiskey.

"Give that man a drink a licker and call the po-leece," Silas says, but he won't talk that way in front of Billy.

The Gullah have their own lingo, a true Creole tongue, the professors say. Approximations of eighteenth-century English and little jewel metaphors strung together on African grammar. It's got a bee-bop rhythm, and when Silas gets a belly full of beer, you might wish he came with subtitles.

"Shot a buck evenin' before last," I said.

It was a nice deer for these scrubby islands, eight tall points with a lot of character, chipped all to hell from tangling with something bigger. I could tell you now about how we hunt deer down here, about getting down in the thicket amongst the copperheads and gators and reading the moon and playing the wind and getting so close you could hit them with a stick, which is the only way you can kill them in the saw palmetto and wax myrtle. How it takes only one shot and how nothing ever goes to waste, but if you've ever done it, you'll know what I mean, and if you haven't, you might never understand.

"Where you get him?" Silas asked.

"'Tween a oak and a pine," I said.

"What you do with the meats?"

"Got some frizz up." I spoke Gullah, too, but only when I got into my whiskey. The words rolled round my tongue like a salty oyster. "Gib some to Miss Suzie and E-vonne and the deacon."

The deacon is Silas's daddy, a pillar in the First Union African Church. He'll stand up each time the offering's taken and pray and wobble and moan till you'd wish the Smithsonian was there to get it all on tape.

> *Amazing sight the Savior stands*
> *He knocks at every do'*

Ten thousand blessing in each hand
To satisfy the po'.

He'll go on like this for a couple of minutes, stringing out couplets and Bible verses like a bluesman. He'll drift off into personal testimony and then buck up and come a-roaring back in a rich baritone.

An when we can't get up
And come to First Union no mo',
Give us a home, Lord, give us a home
In that sacred space where Jesus are.
Amen.

The deacon is Baptist and doesn't cotton much to drinking, but we didn't talk about that right then.

"You ain't bring me broughtus?" Silas asked.

Broughtus means extra, a word the Gullah picked up from their Scot field bosses a long, long time ago. "Slap-outa broughtus 'fore I get to you," I said.

"Well, start on my end of the islunt next time."

It was a ritual. I would lay up meat for the winter, roasts and steaks and sausages and burgers. I would keep on hunting and make the rounds to the shut-ins and to those too old to hunt anymore. The old women knew the routine. I'd drive into their yards, between the flapping clotheslines, the scrabbling chickens, and the milling goats, and they'd come a-running with pots and dishpans.

Silas hunted, too. Most any Saturday, September through March, you could see him pedalling the dirt roads, one hand on the handlebars, the other clutching a bumper jack of a shotgun. "You shoot possum?" I asked.

He shook his head. "Possum eat dead cow and ting."

"I don't like my cow live either," Billy said.

"You shoot coon?"

"Yeah, Bro."

"You shoot squirrel?"

He grunted and nodded.

"Well, how come you won't shoot you a deer?"

Silas took a long pull on his brew. It was getting on down towards the bottom and a whisper of foam ran down his chin. He wagged his head and looked at me sadly. "Well," he said, "they eye too big."

"Looky here," Billy said. "We gonna let them shoot those deer?"

Everybody was riled about the deer on Haig Point. Haig Point was one of those places you can't go unless you belong, an enclave of Philistines from Ohio and New York and Pennsyl-tucky, way up on the north end. They had a gate and a fancy fence and security guards in bwana helmets, and they didn't get down this way much. The deer were chewing up their azaleas and they had applied for a permit to thin them out. Billy does not hunt, but this notion of baiting and night-shooting does and fawns didn't sit well with him either.

"You got money," I said, "looks like you can do anything you want."

"Shoot 'em," Billy said.

"How you talk, man!"

"Shoot the Yankees," Billy said. "Leave them deer alone."

These sentiments were left over from General Sherman,

when he torched every town and farm and school and church from Savannah to Columbia a hundred and forty-odd years ago. It is a long time to hold a grudge, but we got burned out and we still hold it.

"Watch your mouth," Silas said. "The law on the island."

Time was, the steamer captains pulled the whistle cord six times whenever the law was aboard, which would precipitate a great stampede of locals to cover their stills and reefer patches. Now the cops have their own boat, but we have VHF radio and cell phones whenever the weather doesn't block the signal from up along I-95, up where the towers are.

"No they ain't," Billy said. "Their truck's still parked at the landing."

"They fool you," Silas chuckled. "They done been drive Mr. Jimmie skeeter truck."

Done been has no equivalent conjugation in standard English. It's sort of past imperfect—long ongoing past action, continuing now into the present, possibly into the future. The mosquito control truck is a flap-fendered old Ford with a five-horse pump and a tank and a hose and a wand. The cops have commandeered it and have been skulking around in it. They are likely skulking in it tonight and may still be in the morning and even tomorrow afternoon. You might see it coming and pull over to offer Jimmie a brew and—Great Gawd A'mighty—they'd write you up for open container.

The wind sighed and more acorns rattled onto the roof. "Incoming," Billy said again.

"They ticket E-vonne for crowing chicken."

"What you say?" Both of Billy's eyes were working over-time now.

"Sho' 'nuff," Silas said. "Lay in the bush and mark time. Nine o'clock crow, leben o'clock crow. Cost hundred and thirty-two dollar and sebenty-five cent."

Island by island we had seen them come, the golf courses, the tract houses, the highrise apartments they call villas. The farms were gone, the shrimp boats fueling on borrowed money, the free-roaming cattle and wild island ponies just a memory. Yes, they had come to Daufuskie, but there is no bridge and likely never will be, and the development kind of petered out. Even on Haig Point, the most successful in a long string of bankrupt ventures and dashed schemes, there were only a hundred-odd glooming faux-Georgian mansions within two square miles. Haig Pointers were easy to spot. They had this vague shell-shocked look about them. "Hey, they told us this would be the next Martha's Vineyard. What happened?"

They could not move, and we would not move, so there has been an uneasy truce for twenty-odd years now, rich folks in their gated community and the rest of us here on the back of the island.

"Can't a colored woman raise chickens no more?" Billy asked.

"Not if they crow," Silas said.

"End of the world as we know it," Billy said. "Tyler, get me a drink."

Tyler was polishing glasses. His great granddaddy had pioneered here back in the '20s, which makes him only a couple of generations less local than Silas. He'd gone off to school and knocked around the Caribbean a bit, but came back and took up with Beth and she put him to work behind the bar. He's got red hair and wild eyes and a Georgia Bulldog on the front of his shirt. "You sure?"

"You heard me. Whiskey, straight up."

On the other side of the river, in amongst the golf courses and cul-de-sacs, they had been killing deer that way for years—corn baits and quartz lights and high-powered rifles with silencers. But that was over there where it was too jam-up with people and if somebody shot a Mercedes or a Lexus or a neighbor, there'd be a lawsuit. The deer assassins were mostly off-duty SWAT team snipers, hangers-on and wannabe's, looking to pick up extra money. They had their own insurance and they shot them at two in the morning and got the carcasses out before daybreak. If you got up for another Xanax and heard muted gunfire, you could go back to sleep confident the meat would end up on the local food shelf.

But that was over there. Over here we still hunted, and even those who did not expected me to somehow do something about it. I had written a couple of books and had dragged the developers through court a time or two, so I sent off a flurry of letters to the editor and mounted an email campaign and directed the predictable barrage of outrage to the DNR Chief of Wildlife, something he did not entirely appreciate. "It will take us ten days just to deal with this!" he howled.

Meanwhile, suggestions poured in.

"Gather at Haig Point at eight a.m.," one letter said. "Everybody bring a convenient pot, a spoon, and a comfortable jug. Spread out in a long line. At noon walk south. Beat hell out of the pots. All the deer will get the hell out of there and can be shot by anybody needing meat for the table." It was a clever dig at a place where alcohol was a ubiquitous and all-purpose balm for boredom, disappointment and despair.

In time, the DNR sent two biologists. They were mannerly, cautious types in khakis, gub-ment men, conditioned to keep their heads down and their fannies covered. We drove the rutted sandy roads with spotlights, and ten times each mile we turned on the lights. "Visibility!" one would holler. "Ten yards," one would holler back, and the other might yell, "Forty!" I'd write down the numbers and try to sort the bucks from the does and fawns. We had seen sixty-four deer in an eleven-mile criss-cross ramble, and they ran the numbers and told me there was one deer per six point seven acres, or seven hundred and forty-six and one-quarter deer on our five-thousand-acre island.

Anybody who has spent any time in these woods would scoff at that figure, but right then I let it slide. "That too many?" I asked.

"Not really," one replied. "Twice might be."

"How do they look?"

"They look good."

Indeed, they did. If you like to hunt deer, Daufuskie is deer-hunting heaven. Fifteenth of August till the first of the year, no deer tags, no limit on bucks and you can kill two does a day most weekends. The deer are smallish, but they eat mostly acorns and they are fat and sweet and fine.

"Then, why the permit?"

"We hunt deer, too," one of them said, "and we don't like this any more than you do."

"You didn't answer the question," I said.

"What do you propose we do?"

"Deny the permit."

"We've never denied a permit. They might sue."

"Look," I said. "You-all are scientists. I am a poet and maybe a Wobbly, too. Shining deer is against the law. It's always been against the law. We don't shine deer, not because it's illegal, but because it's immoral. A permit won't change that."

The men looked at each other and one of them sighed. In the dashboard half-light, I could not tell which one. They explained. If there were so many deer they were malnourished, they would issue a permit. If there were so many deer they negatively affected their environment, they would issue a permit. Neither being the case, I was beginning to feel better about the evening's activities. But then they told me about something called Social Carrying Capacity.

"You mean," I asked, "if people *think* there are too many deer, you will issue a permit?"

There was a long pause. "That's about it," one said.

"So much for your science," I said. "My poetry still stands."

"We understand how you feel," one of them said. "There's no problem with these deer—people are the problem."

"There are kids here who have never had a chance to hunt. There are old folks here who need the meat."

They said nothing, *didn't crack they teeth*, as the Gullah say.

I went on. "You shoot at a smart buck and miss him, he'll crawl. That's no defense against wolves. That only works for arrows and spears and bullets." It was too much poetry for most anybody, but I was spun up real tight and kept right on at it. "We've evolved together, deer and wolves and people. Deer fed us for half a million years. The wolves followed and picked up the scraps. We caught the pups and made dogs of them."

"Red wolves are back," one said in another brief flash of sympathy. "We turned them loose on Bull Island. They made it through Hurricane Hugo."

"But the deer," I said. "We won't see you shoot them like vermin."

"We saw some over on Haig Point," one of them said. "They were just standing in somebody's yard. Deer don't act like that. Those weren't deer."

"That's what they said about the Vietnamese. They looked funny, they smelled funny, they talked funny. They weren't people, so we didn't mind killing half a million of them."

One of them cut me off. "They are not going to let you into their community to hunt."

"If you deny the permit, they might."

I got them to the landing for the last ferry and then I wandered down to Mudbank Mammy's and met up with Silas and Billy and we all got about half tight as we listened to the acorns roll.

In a couple of days I would get a thick envelope from the DNR. There would be the survey results and a long letter telling me how night-shooting deer on Haig Point would only marginally affect hunting on the remainder of the island. In fact, since they would be shooting only does and fawns, it might make it better for us, since Haig Point bucks would range farther seeking mates.

And later on that same night, Billy would go looking for Jimmie, and there would be some serious jawing on Jimmie's front porch. Besides spraying skeeters, Jimmie is a fireman, and when somebody found an orphan fawn and brought it to the firehouse, Jimmie took it home. He bottle-fed it and named it Rosie, but when it grew nubbins and began nosing the missus around the yard, he started calling it Roosevelt. Roosevelt has since taken to the woods, but shows up each evening for a handful of horse sweet-feed. One day Jimmie wrastled him down and painted Day-Glo orange stripes along his sides, and on his hooves. "Maybe them sons of bitches won't shoot him," he said.

So Jimmie and Billy got into it big time. Jimmie would tell Billy the skeeter truck was a county vehicle and the cops could take it anytime they wanted, and if he had complaints, he should direct them to the sheriff. And Billy would blow and cuss and call the sheriff at midnight and complain most creatively. Though the specifics of that conversation would not be immediately known, it would prompt three cops to come looking for Billy. They would find Beth first.

"Where's Billy?" they'd ask.

"Dunno," she would say. "It ain't my day to take care of him."

But they would find him anyway and they would cuff him and haul him away for making terroristic threats, later reduced to malicious use of an official line. For months afterwards, we would all laugh and call him Osama bin Billy.

But we could not know any of this right then. Tyler brought us another round and Beth gave us each a bowl of gumbo and across the high marsh, the lights of Savannah sadly glimmered off to the southwest. "You gone sue 'em again?" Silas asked.

"Lawyers cost money," I said. "You got any?"

Silas grunted into his beer.

"Looky here," Billy said, "they can always hire a slicker

lawyer than you can. But ain't nobody write like you. Why don't you write it up and get some editor to run it somewheres?" I told him I would try. The seawind freshened and the marshgrass sighed while the palmettoes rattled like sacks of dry bones and handfuls of acorns rattled down upon us all.

"Incoming," Billy said.

The author gratefully acknowledges
prior publication of the following:

River Song – *Beaufort Lowcountry*
Mono and Me – *Sporting Classics*
Of Time and River – *Hilton Head Monthly*
Guiding Light – *Hilton Head Monthly*
Blue Root Real Estate – *Orion Online*
Burying Miss Louise – *Orion*
True North – *Sporting Classics*
Lonesome Woods Like These – *Sporting Classics*
A Windy New Moon Morning – *Shooting Sportsman*
Across the River and into the Pigs – *Sporting Classics*
In the Valley of the Little Knife – *Shooting Sportsman*
Born Meat in a Dry Season – *Gray's Sporting Journal*
A Child in the Way She Shall Go – *Saltwater Sportsman*
Hiroshima on Main – *Orion Online*